看笑話學英文

RALPH L, MARQUARD 編著

任 永 溫 譯

三 民 書 局 印 行

國家圖書館出版品預行編目資料

看笑話學英文／Ralph L. Marquard
編著；任永溫譯. --三版. --臺北市：
三民，民88
　　　面；　　公分
ISBN 957-14-1144-2 (平裝)

1.英國語音　　2.幽默，笑話

805.18　　　　　　　　　84002863

網際網路位址　http://www.sanmin.com.tw

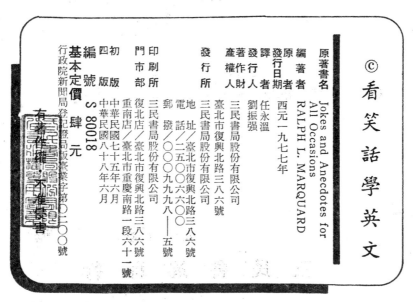

ⓒ 看笑話學英文

原著書名　Jokes and Anecdotes for
　　　　　All Occasions
　　　　　RALPH L. MARQUARD
編　著　者　RALPH L. MARQUARD
譯　　者　任永溫
發行日期　西元一九七七年
發 行 人　劉振強
著作財產權人　三民書局股份有限公司
發 行 所　三民書局股份有限公司
　　　　　　臺北市復興北路三八六號
　　　　　地址／臺北市復興北路三八六號
　　　　　電話／二五○○六六○○
　　　　　郵撥／○○○九九九八──五號
印刷所　三民書局股份有限公司
　　　　　　復興店／臺北市復興北路三八六號
門市部　　重南店／臺北市重慶南路一段六十一號
初　版　中華民國七十五年六月
四　版　中華民國八十八年六月
編　號　S 80018
基本定價　肆　元
行政院新聞局登記證局版臺業字第○二○○號

有著作權 ‧ 不准侵害

ISBN 957-14-1144-2 (平裝)

譯　者　序

本書選譯自 Ralph L. Marquard 所著 "Jokes and Anecdotes"，一小部分是名人軼事。

笑話能表現一個民族的幽默感，也反映着那個民族的習性與生活型態；因為用語大多很通俗，所以讀笑話是學習日常用語的捷徑。

在人際關係中，笑話具有潤滑作用。餐會席上或茶餘酒後，可以製造輕鬆愉快的氣氛。會講笑話的人總是受歡迎的。

原書英文十分精簡、叙事明快、用詞貼切，讀者如能細心玩味，對於英文的潛修，尤其文法方面的體會，應有助益。也是基於此一原因，本書採用中英對照方式，用直譯，並附註釋，來幫助讀者了解和記憶。

讀者或許會發現，在某些句語上，如用意譯或採用較為口語化的句子，可能更為生動活潑；但直譯能更忠于原著，在比照閱讀的時候，會較為省力。

基于文化背景，原書某些笑話，也許不是國人所易於理解的，所以本書只摘譯了原書的三分之一。

書中的笑話，大多有着「即時反應」效果，也有些要細細咀嚼。不過，無論是那種情況，若能令讀者「浮一大白」，為君解頤，則是譯者最感快慰的事。

任　永　溫　民74.5.30
臺北朽廬

CONTENTS

看笑話學英文 目　次

Jokes and Anecdotes

for All Occasions

1. ABSENT-MINDED PROFESSORS

(A)

Oliver Wendell Holmes, American author and physician, was sometimes quite absent-minded.❶

Once Holmes was asked for his ticket on a train, and he could not locate❷ it. He searched through all his pockets and in his briefcase, but was unable to produce the ticket. He became distraught.

The conductor, knowing Mr. Holmes and his sterling reputation, offered reassuringly, "Never mind.❸ When you find your ticket, I am certain you will mail it in."

Holmes didn't seem comforted. "Mr. Conductor," he replied, "the question is not 'Where is my ticket?', but 'Where am I going?'"

註釋: ❶ Absent-minded: 心不在焉的／恍惚的
　　　❷ locate: 找出下落
　　　❸ Never mind: 不要緊

◆◆◆◆◆◆◆◆◆◆◆◆◆◆◆◆◆◆◆◆◆◆◆

(B)

Humanist philosopher Gotthold Lessing was notoriously absent-minded. He once left his Berlin home without taking a key. Returning late that night, he had to rap on

健忘的教授

(A)

　　美國作家兼醫師奧利佛・溫得爾・荷姆斯有時相當心不在焉。

　　有一次荷姆斯搭火車遇到查票，他不知把票放到那裏去了。他找遍了口袋和公事包，但無法出示車票。他煩惱起來。

　　車掌認得荷姆斯先生，也知道他信譽可靠，便想使他安心，建議說：「沒關係。等你找到車票，我想你一定會寄過來的。」

　　荷姆斯好像並未覺得寬慰。「車掌先生，」他回答說：「問題不是我的票在那裏，而是我要到那裏去。」

(B)

　　人類學者又是哲學家的葛托爾・列辛以心不在焉聞名。有一次他沒有帶鑰匙從柏林的家出門，當晚遲了才回去，他只得敲門敲到一個女傭醒來。

the door until one of the maids woke up.

Leaning out a third-floor window into the dark, the maid couldn't make out the figure below, and so shouted, "The professor isn't home."

"Very well," said the forgetful scholar. "Tell him I'll call some other time."

　　女傭倚在三樓的窗上向暗處張望，沒有能辨認出下面的人是誰，便大聲喊着說：「教授不在家。」

　　「好吧！」健忘的學者說：「告訴他，我過些時再來。」

2. AIRPLANES

THE AIRPLANE WAS GOING through some especially turbulent weather, but the pilot knew he had everything under control.❶ He tried to calm the passengers with soothing words spoken over the loudspeaker system. He also asked the stewardesses to reassure the people that everything would be all right.

One little old lady, however, would not be comforted. The stewardess told her how capable the pilot was and how reliable the plane's technology was, but the woman was still sure she'd never see the ground again.

At a loss,❷ the stewardess finally called on the highest court of appeal. "Just trust in Providence," she said soothingly.

The little old lady's eyes opened even wider. "Is it as bad as❸ that?" she asked.

註釋: ❶ under control: 在控制之下
　　　❷ at a loss: 困惑／為難
　　　❸ as bad as: 像□一樣壞

飛　　機

飛機遇到了特別不穩定的氣候，但駕駛員知道一切都在他控制之中。他設法透過擴音器用安慰的話使乘賓鎮定。又讓空中小姐告訴旅客們不會有事。

但有一個小老太太總放不下心。空中小姐對她說駕駛員多麼高明和飛機的製造技術多麼可靠，但她還是覺得一定再也看不到地面了。

空中小姐不知如何是好，最後只得向天求援。「信賴上帝就行了。」她安慰着說。

小老太太把眼睛睜得更大。她問道：「情形有那麼糟嗎？」

3. ANIMAL KINGDOM

(A)

Jones entered the bar and found it empty, except for the bartender❶ and a dog sitting on one of the barstools. The two were engaged in a game of chess.❷ The dog, watching the board intently, wagged his tail when he made a good move❸ and on occasion would bark to indicate "Check!"

　　Finally Jones could no longer contain his astonishment. "Hey," he blurted out, "that's a smart dog you've got there."

　　"He's not so smart!" the bartender replied. "So far I've beat him two out of three."

　　註釋:　❶ bartender: 酒保
　　　　　❷ chess: 西洋象棋
　　　　　❸ make a good move: 下一步好棋

◆◆◆◆◆◆◆◆◆◆◆◆◆◆◆◆◆◆◆◆◆

(B)

As a birthday present, Jim decided to buy his wife a sing-ing canary.❶ He went to great trouble❷ to find one that pleased him, but when he did he brought home to his wife the sweetest-singing canary she'd ever seen or heard in her life.

動 物 國

（A）

　　瓊斯走進酒吧，沒看到客人，只見酒保，另有一隻狗坐在高椅上。這一人一狗正在下西洋象棋。狗聚精會神地望着棋盤，走了一步好棋便搖尾巴，偶爾還會吠叫表示「將軍」。

　　末了瓊斯再也忍不住他的驚奇，脫口說道：「喂！你那隻狗好機靈啊。」

　　酒保回答說：「牠不太機靈！到現在三盤我已經贏了牠兩盤了。」

（B）

　　吉姆決定買一隻會鳴囀的金絲雀，給他太太做生日禮物。他費了很大事，找到一隻他喜歡的，帶回家送給太太，而這一隻却是她一生中從未見過也未聽過的鳴聲最美的金絲雀。

The first day home, the bird warbled beautifully into the night. When Jim's wife fell asleep, lulled by the strains❸ of the golden creature, Jim went to the cage to thank the bird for the rest and joy it gave his wife. But a careful examination of the canary sent Jim back reeling, for the bird was hobbling on one leg.

The next morning, Jim rushed back to the pet store. "What did you sell me here?" he yelled in outrage. "That canary's only got one good leg."

The proprietor eyed him carefully, then replied, "Well, what did you want, a singer or a dancer?"

註釋: ❶ canary: 金絲雀
　　　❷ went to great trouble: 費了大力
　　　❸ strains: 曲調／旋律／歌

到家的第一天，鳥兒顫抖地唱得很悅耳，直到夜晚才歇。吉姆的太太被黃金色小鳥的鳴聲催眠睡着時，吉姆走到鳥籠前謝謝鳥兒給他太太的安窜和喜悅。但是他仔細查看那隻金絲雀之後，不禁躊躇地退了回來，因爲那隻鳥正在用一隻脚跛行。

第二天早晨，吉姆趕忙跑回寵物店，粗暴地喊道:「你賣給我的這個是什麼？」「這隻金絲雀只有一隻脚是好的。」

店主仔細端詳了他一番，然後回答道，「那麼你要的是什麼呢？是唱歌的還是跳舞的？」

4. AUTOMOBILES

(A)

A WOMAN WAS TRYING to maneuver her car out of a parking space.❶ She first crashed into❷ the car ahead, then banged into the car behind, and finally struck a passing delivery truck as she pulled into❸ the street. A policeman who had watched her bumbling efforts approached her. "All right, lady," he demanded, "let's see your license."

"Don't be silly, officer," she replied. "Who'd give *me* a license?"

註釋: ❶ parking space: 停車場
　　　❷ crash into: 碰撞
　　　❸ pull into: 停住

◆◆◆◆◆◆◆◆ ◆◆◆◆◆◆◆◆◆◆

(B)

AN INSURANCE AGENT was teaching his wife how to drive when the brakes❶ of their car failed on a steep downhill grade.

"I can't stop!" shrieked the wife. "What'll I do now?"

"Brace yourself,"❷ her husband advised, "and try to hit something cheap."

註釋: ❶ brakes: 煞車器
　　　❷ brace (oneself) up: 打起精神

汽　車

(A)

　　一個女人要設法把她的車從停車坪開出來。她先撞了前面的車，又砰然一下碰到後面的車，最後她在街道上停住時再撞了一輛送貨車。看着她大費周章的警員走到她身旁說：「得了，太太，給我看看你的駕駛執照吧。」

　　她回答說：「別傻了，警員先生，誰會給我駕駛執照？」

(B)

　　一個保險經紀人正在敎他太太如何開車，在下一個陡坡時煞車不靈了。

　　太太尖叫着說：「我停不住了，現在怎麼辦？」

　　丈夫說：「振作些，盡量撿點便宜的東西撞吧！」

(C)

A WOMAN DRIVING in Brooklyn stopped her car for a red light. However, when the light turned green again, she just stayed right where she was. When the light had changed several times and she still hadn't moved, the traffic policeman❶ finally went over to her and inquired politely, "What's the matter, lady, ain't we got no colors you like?"

註釋:　❶ traffic policeman: 交通警察

◆◆◆◆◆◆◆◆◆◆◆◆◆◆◆◆◆◆◆◆◆◆◆◆

(D)

A TAXI WAS CREEPING slowly through rush-hour traffic, and the passenger was already late. "Please," he told the driver, "can't you go any faster?"

　　"Sure I can," the hack❶ replied. "But I'm not allowed to leave the cab."

註釋:　❶ hack: 計程車司機

(C)

　　一個女人在布魯克林駕車遇到紅燈停了下來。但燈變綠了，她還是停在原處。燈變了好幾次她仍然不動。交通警察最後走到她那裏有禮貌地問道：「怎麼回事啊， 太太， 我們的顏色你沒有一個喜歡的嗎？」

(D)

　　一部計程車在交通擁擠的時候像爬似的緩慢行駛着，而乘客已經遲了。他對司機說：「拜託，你不能再走快點嗎？」

　　司機回答說：「我當然能，可是我是不准離開車的呀。」

(E)

"I'VE GOT TO get rid of Charlie the chauffeur,"❶ complained the husband. "He's nearly killed me four times!"

"Oh!" pleaded his wife, "Give him another chance."❷

註釋: ❶ chauffeur: 爲老闆開轎車的司機

❷ give him another chance: 再給他一次機會

(E)

丈夫埋怨着說:「我非打發司機查理走路不可。 他已經有四次幾乎讓我送命了。」

太太懇求說: 「啊，再給他一次機會吧。」

5. BEAUTY

(A)

AN ACTOR at a dinner party gazed admiringly at a beautiful starlet seated at the next table. Not knowing who she was, the actor sought enlightenment❶ from his friend Beatrice Lillie, comedienne❷ and stage star, who was at the same table as the starlet.

He sent this message: "My God, Bea, who is that incredibly gorgeous creature at your table?"

Indignantly, Miss Lillie scribbled❸ a retort and the waiter took it over. The terse❹ reply said, *"Me!"*

註釋: ❶ enlightenment: 啓發
　　　❷ comedienne: 喜劇女演員
　　　❸ scribble: 潦草地寫
　　　❹ terse: 簡明的

美　　艷

(A)

　　一個演員在一次晚餐會上讚嘆地注視着坐在鄰桌的一個小明星。因爲不知道她是誰，演員便去請敎與小明星同坐一桌的朋友舞臺喜劇明星比阿特麗斯‧李莉。

　　他遞了一張便條：「我的上帝，　比，　你桌上那個耀眼的人兒是誰？」

　　李莉小姐很生氣，草草地寫了一個回條，由侍者送了過去。那簡單的答覆是：「我！」

(B)

The mother had allowed her youngest daughter to watch her while she went through❶ her beauty ritual one evening. The little girl was fascinated with all the jars and creams and lotions; she asked countless questions.

At one point, the woman dipped her fingers into a jar of cold cream and spread the cream on her face. "What's that for, Mommy?" asked her daughter.

"Why, this is to make me beautiful," the woman replied. Then she concentrated on removing every last trace of it with tissues. When she was through, she gazed at her clean face in the mirror.

"Didn't work,❷ did it?" observed her innocent daughter.

註釋: ❶ go through: 通過／經過／做完
　　　 ❷ work: 有效／發生作用

(B)

　　一天晚上媽媽准許小女兒在一旁看她做例行的美容步驟。小女孩對於一大堆瓶瓶罐罐和面霜化粧水着了迷；她問了無數的問題。

　　有一個階段，婦人把手指插入冷霜瓶，把冷霜擦滿在臉上。女兒問道：「媽，那是做什麼？」

　　婦人回答說：「噢，這是讓我漂亮的。」然後她聚精會神用化粧紙把冷霜絲毫不剩擦抹乾淨。擦完後，她對鏡細看她乾淨的面孔。

　　天眞的女兒發表意見說：「沒用，是吧？」

6. BIRTHDAYS & ANNIVERSARIES

FOR HIS BIRTHDAY, Mrs. Finkelstein gave her grown-up son Charlie two Dior ties. One was red and the other blue.

On his next visit to his mother, Charlie put on❶ the red tie and strode into the apartment.

His mother took one look at him and sighed, "Ah! The blue one you didn't like."

註釋: ❶ put on: 戴／穿

生日與周年紀念

　　芬克爾斯坦太太送了兩條狄奧牌領帶給她成年的兒子查理過生日。一條紅色一條藍色。

　　查理下一次去看他母親時，繫了紅領帶走進公寓。

　　他母親望了他一眼，然後嘆氣說：「唉，那條藍的你不喜歡。」

7. BORROWING & LENDING

(A)

A butcher was going over❶ his account books and found that Mrs. Levy owed him a sizable sum of money. He called her on the phone several times, but could never get in touch,❷ so he decided to send her a letter.

"Dear Mrs. Levy," he wrote, "please pay up❸ the money that you owe me."

The next week, he received a reply in the mail: "I can't pay right now, but please send me two good chickens, four pounds of hamburger, and six steaks."

The butcher was angry. He wrote again: "Dear Mrs. Levy: I will send your order when you pay up your account."

The reply came the next day: "I can't wait that long!"

註釋: ❶ go over: 檢查
　　　❷ get in touch: 接觸／連絡
　　　❸ pay up: 付清

借 與 貸

(A)

　　一個肉販查看帳簿，發現雷維太太欠了他相當大的一筆錢。他給她打了幾次電話，但都連絡不上，因此決定寫一封信。

　　「親愛的雷維太太，」他寫道：「請你把欠我的錢付清。」

　　過了一個禮拜，他接到一封回信：「現在我不能付，但要請你送兩隻上好的雞、四磅碎牛肉和六塊牛排肉給我。」

　　肉販生氣了。他再寫信說：「雷維太太：你付清帳我就送貨給你。」

　　第二天回信來了：「我不能等那麼久！」

(B)

The grocer's son had come home from his first year at the university and was anxious to discuss serious subjects with his father. The grocer was pleased.

"Father," the idealistic young man expounded, "it seems to me the world is crazy. The rich, who have lots of money, buy on credit,❶ but the poor, who don't have a cent, must pay cash. Don't you think it should be the other way around?❷ The rich, having money, should pay cash; and the poor, having none, should get credit."

The grocer smiled at his son's lack of business acumen. "But," he pointed out, "if a storekeeper gave credit to the poor, he himself would soon become poor."

"So what?" countered the college boy. "Then he would be able to buy on credit, too!"

註釋: ❶ on credit: 賒帳／信用貸款
　　　❷ the other way round: 相反的／倒過來

（B）

　　雜貨商的兒子上了一年大學回到家，想和他父親討論正經問題。雜貨商很高興。

　　「爸爸，」理想主義的兒子說：「我覺得這世界簡直是沒有道理極了。潤人，有很多錢，買東西賒帳，而窮人，一分錢沒有，倒非付現不可。你不覺得應該反過來嗎？潤人有錢應該付現；窮人沒有錢應該賒帳。」

　　雜貨商笑他兒子缺乏生意眼：「如果一個店舖老闆賒帳給窮人，他自己不久也會變成窮人了。」

　　「那又有什麼關係呢？」大學生反駁說：「那麼他買東西也可以賒帳了。」

8. BUREAUCRACY

The head of one Washington administration was approached by his secretary. "Sir," she said, "our files are becoming overcrowded."

"What do you suggest we do?" asked the busy administrator.

"I think we ought to destroy all correspondence more than six years old." answered the secretary.

"By all means,"● the prudent bureaucrat responded, "go right ahead. But be sure to make copies."

註釋: ● by all means: 好的／當然

官　　僚

　　一位華盛頓機關主管的秘書走過來對他說：「長官，我們的卷宗越積越多了。」

　　忙碌的主管問道：「你認為我們該怎麼辦呢？」

　　秘書回答說：「我想我們該把存了六年的信件全部銷毀。」

　　「當然！」謹慎的官僚說道：「馬上就辦吧！但一定要留副本啊！」

9. BUSINESS

(A)

The prospect of following in his father's footsteps and becoming a poor farmer did not appeal to❶ young Smith. So, he acted quickly when the job of sexton at the local church fell vacant and was first in line with his application. But the minister was forced to refuse him, for the fact was Smith could neither read nor write.

Smith moved to the city, found a job, and invested wisely. By the time he reached 40, he had become a multi-millionaire.❷

When Smith returned to his home town, it came as a shock to everyone that the prosperous businessman still could neither read nor write.

"It is amazing, Mr. Smith," an old friend said to him, "that you have accomplished so much without being able to read or write. Can you imagine what you would be today if you could?"

"Certainly," Smith chuckled. "A church sexton."

註釋： ❶ appeal to: 投合（心意）／起共鳴
　　　 ❷ multi-millionaire: 大富豪／千萬富翁

生　意　經

（A）

　　年輕的史密斯無意追隨他父親的足跡，將來做一個貧窮的農夫。因此地方上的教堂司事出缺時，他便迅速採取行動，第一個跑去應徵。但是由於史密斯既不識字又不會書寫，牧師不得不拒絕。

　　史密斯遷居到城市，找到一份工作，精明地去投資。到四十歲的時候，他已經成為一位千萬富翁了。

　　當史密斯回到故鄉，人們得知這位發達的商人還是不會閱讀寫字時，都大為驚訝。

　　「史密斯先生！」一位老朋友對他說：「你不會讀又不會寫還能有這麼大的成就，真令人驚奇。如果你會讀會寫，你想像今天會做什麼呢？」

　　「當然，」史密斯呵呵笑著說：「教堂的司事。」

(B)

The bald❶ headed barber was trying to sell his customer a bottle of hair tonic.

"But how can you sell this stuff when you yourself are bald!" challenged the customer.

"Nothing wrong with that!" came the reply. "There are 10,000 guys selling brassieres!"❷

註釋: ❶ bald: 禿的
　　　❷ brassieres: 奶罩

◆◆◆◆◆◆◆◆◆◆◆◆◆◆◆◆◆◆◆◆◆◆

(C)

THE YOUNG SON of a garment maker was in school one day when the teacher asked him to name the four seasons.

The boy stood up and said, "I only know two: busy and slack!"

◆◆◆◆◆◆◆◆◆◆◆◆◆◆◆◆◆◆◆◆◆◆

(D)

THE PRESIDENT and chairman of the board❶ of one of the nation's largest corporations was conducting an annual meeting of the stockholders. He presented the board's officers to the gathering and then began the meeting's business.

(B)

禿頭的理髮師向顧客兜售一瓶養髮劑。

顧客反問道：「你自己禿頭，怎麼還能賣這種東西！」

「這一點都沒有什麼不對勁啊！」答話來了。「有一萬個男人在賣奶罩呢！」

(C)

一個成衣商的年幼兒子有一天到學校，老師要他說出四季的名字。

男孩站起來說：「我只知道兩個：旺季和淡季！」

(D)

國內一家大公司的董事長正在主持一次股東年會。他把董事會的職員介紹給大家之後，便開始進行會議的事務。

"Wait a minute," shouted a voice from the audience. "Who are you and what do you do for this company?"

The president was surprised, but he remained composed.❷ "I'm your chairman," he said calmly. "And, of course, you know the duties of a chairman. I'd say he was roughly the equivalent of parsley❸ on a platter of fish."

註釋: ❶ chairman of the board: 董事長
　　　❷ composed: 沈着／鎮定
　　　❸ parsley: 荷蘭芹／香菜

「等一下，」聽眾裏有一個聲音喊道：「你是誰？替公司做什麼事？」

董事長吃了一驚，但還沈得住氣。「我是你們的董事長，」他鎮定地說：「你們當然知道一個董事長的職務。我可以說他差不多就等於一盤魚裏的香菜。」

10. CHARITY & FUND RAISING

(A)

A wealthy New York businessman died and was met at the gates of heaven.

"Who are you?" asked an assistant angel.

"I'm a businessman."

"Well, what have you done to deserve a place in heaven?"

"Why, just the other day I saw a blind man on Broadway and gave him a dime."

"Is that all?"

"Well, last week when I was walking on Wall Street I met a wino❶ who was half frozen to death. I gave him fifteen cents."

The angel turned to the bookkeeper. "Is that in the records?"

The bookkeeper thumbed through the pages of his ledger and confirmed the businessman's claim.

"What else have you done?" the heavenly interrogator continued.

"That's all I can think of at the moment," the man shrugged.

"What do you think we ought to do with this guy?" the angel asked the bookkeeper.

慈善與基金籌募

（A）

一個紐約的富商死後到了天堂的大門前。

「你是誰？」一位助理天使問道。
「我是商人。」
「你做了什麼事夠資格進天堂？」

「對了！那天我在百老滙看到一個瞎子，給了他一毛錢。」

「只有這點嗎？」
「噢！上禮拜我走到華爾街上，遇見一個凍得半死的酒鬼。我給了他一毛五。」

天使轉向管記錄的說：「記錄裏有這回事嗎？」

記錄員翻了翻簿子，確認了商人所說的話。

「你還做了些什麼呢？」天使繼續質詢說。

「目前我能想到的只有這些了。」那人聳聳肩說。

「你覺得我們應該怎樣處置這傢伙呢？」天使問記錄員說。

"Give him back his quarter and tell him to go to hell!"❷

註釋: ❶ wino: 酒鬼
❷ go to hell: 滾蛋

◆◆◆◆◆◆◆◆◆◆◆◆◆◆◆◆◆◆◆◆

(B)

It is said that experience is the best teacher of all. A minister in a parish of various income levels believed this maxim,❶ and he had to find a way to induce❷ the wealthier congregants to give more money. He devised a clever plan.

He made an appointment to see Mr. Walker, a millionaire who was notoriously❸ stingy,❹ on a cold November day. The minister was greeted graciously by his host and offered some hot tea to warm himself. He mentioned nothing of the purpose of the visit, speaking only generally about the church. Then he rose to leave.

Buttoning his thick woolen overcoat, the minister asked if Mr. Walker would see him to the front door. The front hall was not heated, but Mr. Walker didn't take a sweater—he thought he'd return to his living room momentarily. But the minister stood by the open front door for fifteen minutes, speaking only of inconsequential❺ things.

「還給他兩毛五，叫他滾！」

(B)

　　人們說經驗是最好的老師。一個有各種不同水平收入的教區的牧師相信這格言，而且要想個方法使富有的會眾多出些錢。他想出了一個聰明的辦法。

　　一個十一月的冷天，他約定去看華克先生，一個出名吝嗇的百萬富翁。主人慇勤地招待牧師，並且請他喝熱茶暖暖身。牧師對於他來訪的目的一字不提，只是談了一些普通的教會的事，然後就站起來要走。

　　牧師扣好他厚大衣的鈕扣，問華克先生可否送他到大門口。玄關沒有生火，而華克先生又沒有穿毛衣——他想他馬上就會回到他的起坐間了。但是牧師站在打開的大門旁邊十五分鐘，只講一些無關緊要的事。

Mr. Walker began to shiver with the cold. He tried to close the door and invite the minister back to the living room, but the pastor said nonsense, he'd be leaving in a minute. The host began to feel he would turn blue.

Finally, he could be polite no longer. "If you do not tell me what you want," he said, "I'll freeze to death. I'm so cold my blood has almost stopped flowing in my veins."

"I'll tell you what I came for," the minister said honestly. "I need fifty dollars to buy coal for some poor people."

"Here's the money," said the bewildered millionaire. "But why couldn't you tell me this inside? Why did you have to take me out into the cold hall?"

The minister explained his reasoning. "Inside, perhaps you would not have realized what it means to be cold. Now, you too have a taste of it."

註釋: ❶ maxim: 格言
　　　 ❷ induce: 勸使
　　　 ❸ notoriously: 聲名狼藉／有名的 (通常用於壞的方面)
　　　 ❹ stingy: 吝嗇的
　　　 ❺ inconsequential: 不重要的

◆◆◆◆◆◆◆◆◆◆◆◆◆◆◆◆◆

(C)

"See here, Mr. Gottlieb," asserted the high-powered voice, "we have asked you time and again for a contribu-

　　華克先生開始冷得發抖了。他想關上門請牧師回到起坐間，但牧師說何必呢，他一下就走的。主人開始感覺凍得發青了。

　　最後他不能再講禮貌了。「如果你不告訴我你要什麽，」他說：「我要凍死了。我冷得好像血管裏的血都快停止流動了。」

　　「我告訴你我是爲什麽來的吧，」牧師老實說：「我 需要五十塊錢買煤給一些窮人。」

　　「錢在這兒，」莫明所以的百萬富翁說：「不過你爲什麽不在裏面告訴我呢？爲什麽要把我帶到這麽冷的玄關來呢？」

　　牧師解釋他的道理說：「在裏面，　你大概不會瞭解冷是什麽。現在你也嚐到冷的滋味了。」

(C)

　　「哥特利布先生，　你說說看，」一個人大聲說道：「我們已經好幾次請你捐款，你每次都拒絕了。但是你有三棟房子，四

tion, and you've refused every time. Yet you have three homes, four elegant cars, you own a chain of department stores, and belong to two country clubs.❶ So how can you turn us down?"❷

Gottlieb's tone was equally strong. "Madam, have you any idea of the situation in my family? My mother has a heart disease so severe she must remain in the hospital. My brother is indigent and on relief.❸ My aged uncle is a cripple who can't support himself." "So," Gottlieb continued, "if I don't give any of them any money, why should I give anything to you?"

註釋: ❶ country club: 田園俱樂部 (有運動場所、食堂等設施)
❷ turn down: 拒絕／駁回
❸ on relief: 接受政府救濟

輛高雅的車，一串連鎖百貨公司，並且參加了兩個田園俱樂部。
你怎麼還能拒絕我們呢？」

　　哥特利布的聲調同樣地強而有力。「太太，你想得到我家
裏是什麼情形嗎？我母親有心臟病，嚴重到必須住醫院。我兄
弟窮困，在接受政府救濟。我年老的伯父是個殘廢，不能自食
其力。」哥特利布繼續說：「所以，如果我一點錢也不給他們，
我為什麼要給你們呢？」

11. COURTING & SEDUCTION

(A)

Stanley was already in his twenties and he had never had a date with a girl, so his older brother decided it was time to do something about it. He arranged a blind date❶ for Stanley with a nice young girl who was just as innocent as Stanley. But Stanley was very nervous. His hands became clammy❷ and his tongue felt stiff as marble.

"Help me, Mark. I don't know how to talk to girls. How can I be a good conversationalist like you?" asked Stanley.

Mark had some advice to offer. "Listen, Stan," he said, "I have a formula❸ that never fails. Talk about family, food, and philosophy. Any of those topics is guaranteed to get a girl talking. Try it! I'm sure it'll work."

So Stanley went to meet the girl. She was pretty and shy. Stanley wanted very much to make a good impression. He thought of his brother's advice. First, he'd talk family.

"Tell me," he began nervously, "do you have a brother?"

"No!" came the girl's swift reply.

"Oh." Stanley was stymied, so he moved to the topic of food. "Do you like noodles?"

"No!" she said again.

求愛與引誘

(A)

　　史丹利已經二十幾歲，還從未和女孩子約會過，因此他哥哥確定到了該想想辦法的時候了。他爲史丹利和一個同史丹利一樣天眞的女孩安排了一次約會。但史丹利很緊張。他的手變得濕濕黏黏，舌頭也感覺硬得像塊石頭。

　　「幫幫忙，馬克。我不知道怎樣同女孩講話。如何才能像你一樣的健談呢？」史丹利問道。

　　馬克提供了一些建議。「聽着，史丹，」他說：「我有個公式從不會失敗的。講家人、吃的東西和愛好。這些話題任何一個都保證會讓女孩子講話。試試看！我想一定管用。」

　　於是史丹利就去會那女孩了。她漂亮而害羞。史丹利非常想給對方一個好印象。他想到了哥哥的建議。第一，他要講家人。
　　「告訴我，」他膽怯地開始道：「你有兄弟嗎？」

　　「沒有！」女孩的回答來得迅速。
　　「噢，」史丹利碰了壁，便轉到食物的話題。「你喜歡吃麵嗎？」
　　「不！」她又說了。

But Stanley wasn't at a loss. He remembered his brother's advice. He'd talk philosophy. "Say," he said, "if you had a brother, would he like noodles?"

註釋:　❶ blind date: 由第三者介紹彼此不相識男女間的約會
　　　❷ clammy: 發黏的／濕冷的
　　　❸ formula: 公式

◆◆◆◆◆◆◆◆◆◆◆◆◆◆◆◆◆◆

(B)

Stopping in an unfamiliar barber shop for a shave, a young playboy took a fancy to❶ the manicure❷ girl and suggested dinner and a show that evening.

"I don't think I ought to," the girl demurred.❸ "I'm married."

"Why don't you ask your husband," the playboy suggested. "I'm sure he wouldn't object."

"You can ask him yourself," the girl shrugged. "He's shaving you."

註釋:　❶ take a fancy to: 愛好，愛上
　　　❷ manicure: 修指甲
　　　❸ demur: 反對

◆◆◆◆◆◆◆◆◆◆◆◆◆◆◆◆◆◆

可是史丹利並沒有被難倒。他記得哥哥的建議。他要講愛好。「那麼，」他說：「假如你有個兄弟，他會喜歡吃麵嗎？」

(B)

一個年輕的花花大少在一家陌生的理髮店停下來刮鬍鬚，看上了修指甲的女郎，提議晚上去吃飯看表演。

「我想我不該去，」女郎反對說：「我是結過婚的。」

「那你爲什麼不問問你丈夫呢？」花花大少提議說：「我想他一定不會反對的。」

「你自己問他好了，」女郎聳聳肩。「他在替你刮鬍子呢。」

(C)

THIS STORY CONCERNS a particularly persistent suitor.❶ He lived in Chicago and courted a girl in Oshkosh for two years.

Things somehow went wrong❷ and she wouldn't see him any longer. So he took to the mails and he sent her a special delivery letter three times a day for 33 days.

On the 34th day, his strategy❸ produced results. The girl eloped❹ with the mailman.

註釋:　❶ suitor: 求婚者
　　　　❷ went (go) wrong: 出毛病／出差錯
　　　　❸ strategy: 策略
　　　　❹ elope: 私奔

◆◆◆◆◆◆◆◆◆◆◆◆◆◆◆◆◆◆◆◆◆

(D)

A YOUNG FELLOW brought home his bride-to-be to be appraised❶ by his father.

The older man was flabbergasted,❷ chagrined,❸ and embarrassed. He took the boy aside into the next room and whispered in his ear, "I never saw such a homely❹ girl. She's got hair on her chin; her eyes are watching each other; and her teeth are crooked."

(C)

這是關於一個特別執拗的求婚者的故事。他住在芝加哥，向一個奧西柯西的女郎求愛兩年。

不知怎的事情出了差錯，她不願再和他見面。於是他開始寫信，一天寄給她三封掛號信，寄了三十三天。

在第三十四天，他的策略產生了結果。女郎同郵差私奔了。

(D)

一個小伙子把他的準新娘帶回家請他父親評定。

老人看了大吃一驚，旣懊惱又感覺爲難。他把年輕人拉開，走進隔壁房間輕聲在他耳邊說：「我沒見過這麼醜的女孩。她下巴上長毛；眼睛鬥雞；牙齒是歪歪扭扭的。」

"Pop, you don't have to whisper," the son replied. "You can talk louder. She's deaf too."

註釋：　❶ appraise: 評價／品定
　　　　❷ flabbergasted: 使大吃一驚
　　　　❸ chagrin: 懊惱
　　　　❹ homely: 醜陋的

「爸，你不必小聲說話，」兒子回答道：「你可以說響一點，她還是個聾子啊。」

12. CUSTOMERS

(A)

MRS. KOHANSKY WENT to her butcher of many years and said, "Bernie, today I need a beautiful chicken, maybe four pounds."

Bernie pointed out three chickens in the display counter, but Mrs. Kohansky turned up her nose at❶ all of them. "I asked for a *beautiful* chicken," she sniffed.

So Bernie went to the back of the store, and from his refrigerator room he extracted❷ an especially plump fowl. He brought it forward with pride.

The lady was cautious. She took the chicken and slowly began to examine each part with her fingers—lifting the wings, feeling the breast, and groping❸ inside the cavity.❹

Finally, the butcher's patience waned. "Tell me, Mrs. Kohansky," he demanded, "do you think *you* could pass such a test?"

註釋:　❶ turn up one's nose at: 瞧不起／鄙視

　　　❷ extract: 抽出

　　　❸ grope: 摸索

　　　❹ cavity: 腔

顧　　客

(A)

柯韓斯基太太到她多年的熟肉店去說：「伯尼，　今天我要一隻漂亮的雞，大概四磅左右。」

伯尼指了指陳列貨色櫃裏的三隻雞，但柯韓斯基太太都看不中。「我要的是一隻漂亮的雞，」她不屑地說。

於是伯尼走到店後面，從他的冷藏室取出一隻特別肥的肉雞。他得意地把雞拿到前面。

婦人蠻慎重。她拿着雞，開始用手指慢慢地檢查每一部分——拉起翅膀，按按胸脯，又去掏摸腔內。

後來，肉販忍耐不住了。「告訴我，柯韓斯基太太，」他問道：「你想你自已能通過這種樣子的檢驗嗎？」

(B)

IT WAS A BROILING day in July. Mrs. Finkelstein went into a store to buy a fan.

"What kind fan do you want?" asked Levy, the storekeeper. "We have fans for a nickel, for a quarter, and for a dollar."

"So give me one for a nickel," said Mrs. Finkelstein.

"O.K."said Levy, as he handed her a thin Japanese paper fan.

In 10 minutes, Mrs. Finkelstein was back. "Look what trash❶ you sold me!" she shouted. "The fan broke."

"It did?" said Levy. "And how did you use it?"

"How did I use it?" replied Mrs. Finkelstein. "How do you use a fan? I held it in my hand, and I waved it back and forth❷ in front of❸ my face. Did you ever?"

"Oh no!" explained Levy, "With a five-cent fan, you got to hold it still, in both hands, like this, and wave your head back and forth in front of it."

註釋: ❶ trash: 廢物／垃圾
　　　❷ back and forth: 前後來回
　　　❸ in front of: 在□之前

(B)

　　那是一個酷熱的七月天。芬克爾斯坦太太走進一間店舖去買扇子。

　　「你要那一種扇子？」店員列維問道：「我們有五分錢的，兩毛五的，和一塊錢的扇子。」

　　「那就給我一把五分錢的吧，」芬克爾斯坦太太說。

　　「好，」列維說着，遞了一把薄薄的日本紙扇給她。

　　不到十分鐘，芬克爾斯坦太太就回來了。「看看你賣給我的是什麼爛貨！」她叫喊着說：「扇子已經壞了。」

　　「是嗎？」列維說：「那你是怎麼用它的呢？」

　　「我怎麼用它？」芬克爾斯坦太太回答說：「你怎麼用扇子啊？我是把它拿在手裏，在我面前來回搖動的呀。你沒有用過嗎？」

　　「噢不行啊！」列維解釋說：「一把五分錢的扇子，你得用兩隻手拿穩，像這樣，然後在扇子前面把你的頭來回搖動。」

13. DEATH & MOURNING

(A)

Two Scotsmen and a Jew gathered at the casket of a friend. The first Scotsman made a little speech.

"As you well know, my friends, I am a thrifty soul, but there is a legend in my family that if one places a wee bit❶ of money in the casket to be buried with the body, it will ease the departed's way into the next world. For the sake of❷ our friend, I place ten dollars in the casket with him."

The second Scotsman didn't want to look cheap, so he, too, took out a ten-dollar bill and dropped it into the casket.

Then the Jew moved forward. "Do you think I won't join in this kind deed?" he asked. Whereupon he took out his checkbook and wrote a check for thirty dollars. He placed it in the dead man's hand, and took the two ten-dollar bills as change.❸

註釋:　❶ a wee bit: 只有一點點
　　　　❷ for the sake of: 爲了
　　　　❸ change: 找頭／零錢

喪事與弔喪

(A)

　　兩個蘇格蘭人和一個猶太人聚在一個朋友的棺木旁邊。第一個蘇格蘭人說了一段簡短的話。

　　「朋友們，你們很知道，我是一個節儉的人，但我家有個傳說講如果放一點點錢在棺木裏，可以讓死者順利走進下一個世界。為了我們的朋友，我在他棺木裏放十塊錢。」

　　第二個蘇格蘭人不願顯得寒酸，所以他也拿出一張十元鈔票，丟進棺木。

　　然後猶太人走到前面。「你們以為我不會參加這個善舉嗎？」他問道。於是他拿出支票簿，開了一張三十元的支票。他把支票放在死者手裏，找回了兩張十元鈔票。

(B)

DEEP IN THE Tennessee hills, a farmer's mule❶ kicked his mother-in-law❷ to death. An enormous crowd of men turned out for the funeral. The minister, examining the crowd outside the church, commented to a farmer friend, "This old lady must have been mighty popular. Just look at how many people left their work to come to her funeral."

"They're not here for the funeral," snickered❸ the friend. "They're here to buy the mule."

註釋:　❶ mule: 騾子
　　　　❷ mother-in-law: 岳母
　　　　❸ snicker: 偷偷地笑

（B）

　　在田納西的深山裏，一個農夫的騾子把他岳母踢死了。安葬時來了一大群人。牧師看到敎堂外面的人群，向一個農夫朋友說：「這位老太太人緣一定很好。看看有多少人放下工作到她的葬禮來。」

　　「他們不是爲葬禮到這兒來的。他們是來買那隻騾子的。」朋友吃吃地竊笑着說。

14. DOCTORS & MEDICINE

(A)

The poor tailor was beside himself.❶ His wife was sick and perhaps dying. He called on the only doctor nearby.

"Please, save my wife, doctor! I'll pay anything!"

"But what if I can't cure her?" asked the doctor.

"I'll pay whether you cure her or kill her, if only you'll come right away!"

So the doctor promptly visited the woman, but within a week, she died. Soon a bill arrived charging the tailor a tremendous fee. The tailor couldn't hope to pay, so he asked the doctor to appear with him before the local rabbi❷ to arbitrate the case.

"He agreed to pay me for treating his wife," stated the physician, "whether I cured her or killed her."

The rabbi was thoughtful. "Well, did you cure her?" he asked.

醫 生 與 藥

（A）

　　可憐的裁縫慌了手腳。他的妻子生病，可能快要死了。他跑去找附近唯一的一位醫生。

　　「大夫，請救救我太太！多少錢我都付！」

　　「可是如果我不能治好她怎麼辦？」醫生問道。

　　「只要你馬上來，不管你治好她還是治壞她我都付錢！」

　　於是醫生很快去看那女人，但不到一星期，她就死了。不久來了一張帳單，要裁縫付一筆驚人的費用。裁縫沒有希望付得起，便請醫生同他一起到當地猶太教的牧師面前仲裁這件事。

　　「他答允付我治他太太的費用，」醫師說：「不管我治好她還是治壞她。」

　　牧師深思了一下。「那麼，你治好她了嗎？」他問道。

"No," admitted the doctor.

"And did you kill her?"

"I certainly did not!" expostulated❸ the physician.

"In that case,"❹ the rabbi said with finality, "You have no grounds on which to base a fee."

註釋: ❶ beside oneself: 喪失自主
   ❷ rabbi: 猶太教會的牧師
   ❸ expostulate: 反駁
   ❹ in that case: 假使那樣

◆◆◆◆◆◆◆◆◆◆◆◆◆◆◆◆◆◆◆◆

(B)

Mr. Carson placed a frantic❶ phone call to his doctor and explained that his wife, who always slept with her mouth open, had a mouse caught in her throat.

"I'll be over in a few minutes," said the doctor. "In the meantime, try waving a piece of cheese in front of her mouth."

When the doctor reached the Carson apartment, he found Mr. Carson waving a five-pound haddock❷ in front of his wife's face.

"What are you doing?" exclaimed the doctor. "I told you to wave a piece of cheese. Mice don't like haddock",

「沒有！」醫生承認道。

「你治死她了？」

「我當然沒有！」醫生反駁地說。

「那樣的話，」牧師斷然說：「你就沒有收費的根據了。」

(B)

　　卡生先生瘋了似的打電話給他的醫生，告訴醫生他經常張嘴睡覺的太太喉嚨裏卡了一隻老鼠。

　　「我過幾分鐘就來，」醫生說：「目前，你先試試拿一片乳酪在你太太的嘴前面搖晃。」

　　當醫生到達卡生的公寓時，他看見卡生先生正拿着一條五磅的鱈魚在他太太面前搖晃。

　　「你在做什麼啊？」醫生叫道：「我是告訴你搖一片乳酪。老鼠不喜歡鱈魚的。」

"I know," Mr. Carson gasped, "But I've got to get the cat out first."

註釋: ❶ frantic: 瘋狂似的
　　　❷ haddock: 鱈的一種

◆◆◆◆◆◆◆◆◆◆◆◆◆◆◆◆◆◆◆

(C)

THE AMBASSADOR'S WIFE was walking to a luncheon one day when she noticed an accident that had occurred at the street corner ahead. Suddenly, she was grateful for the first-aid course she'd recently attended.

As she told her husband later, "I was crossing the street when I saw the poor man lying there. He had been hit by a cab and was in a bad way.❶

"Then all my first aid❷ came back to me, and I stooped right down and put my head between my knees to keep from fainting."

註釋: ❶ in a bad way: 情形不好
　　　❷ first aid: 急救

◆◆◆◆◆◆◆◆◆◆◆◆◆◆◆◆◆◆◆

「我知道，」卡生先生喘着氣說：「可是我得先把貓弄出來呀。」

(C)

大使夫人有一天步行去參加一個午餐會，在前面道路轉角的地方看到發生了事故。她突然覺得很高興最近參加了急救課程講習。

後來她告訴她丈夫說：「過街時我看見可憐的男人躺在那裏。他被計程車撞了，情形不好。」

「那時所有我的急救知識都回來了。我馬上彎下身，把頭夾在兩腿的膝蓋中間，以免昏倒。」

(D)

A MAN CAME to a doctor complaining that he had an uncontrollable cough. The doctor gave him a bottle of castor oil and said, "Go home and drink down the entire bottle, and come back tomorrow."

When the patient came back next day, the doctor asked, "Did you take the castor oil?"

The man answered "Yes." The doctor then continued, "Do you still cough?"

The patient said, "Yes, I continue to cough."

The doctor gave him a second bottle of castor oil❶ and said, "Take this, and come back tomorrow."

The next day, the man returned. The doctor asked him, "Do you still cough?"

And the patient said, "Yes, I still cough regularly."

The doctor then gave him yet another bottle of castor oil and said, "Drink this entire bottle tonight and come back tomorrow morning."

The patient returned, and the doctor looked at the poor wretch❷ and said, "Do you cough now?"

The patient quiveringly answered, "I don't cough any more—I'm afraid to."

註釋: ❶ castor oil: 蓖麻子油
　　　❷ wretch: 可憐的人

(D)

　　一個人到醫生的地方訴說他咳嗽咳得無法抑制。醫生給了他一瓶蓖麻子油說：「回家把整瓶喝下去，明天再來。」

　　病人第二天再來時，醫生問道：「你吃了蓖麻子油嗎？」

　　那個人回答：「是。」醫生接着說：「那你還咳嗎？」

　　病人說：「是，我還在咳。」
　　醫生給了他第二瓶蓖麻子油說：「吃了這瓶，明天再來。」

　　第二天那人又來了。醫生問他：「你還咳嗎？」

　　病人說：「是，我還經常咳。」
　　醫生於是又給了他一瓶蓖麻子油說：「今晚把這個整瓶喝了，明天早上再來。」

　　病人回來了。醫生望着那可憐的傢伙說：「你現在還咳嗎？」
　　病人顫抖著回答說：「我不再咳了—我怕咳了。」

(E)

"NOW TELL ME," said the Doctor, "do you always stutter?❶"

The patient thought for a while and then said, "N-n-no d-d-doc. J-j-just when I t-t-talk!"

註釋: ❶ stutter: 口吃

◆❖◆❖◆❖◆❖◆❖◆❖◆❖◆❖◆❖◆◆

(F)

SIMPSON, BOTHERED BY a sore throat, went to his doctor for a prescription.❶ The doctor's pretty nurse answered the bell.

"Is the doctor in?" Simpson asked in a hoarse❷ whisper.

"No, come in!" the young lady whispered back.

註釋: ❶ prescription: 處方
　　　❷ hoarse: 沙啞的

◆❖◆❖◆❖◆❖◆❖◆❖◆❖◆❖◆❖◆◆

(E)

「來告訴我，」醫生說：「他老是口吃嗎？」

病人想了一會，然後說：「不—不—不醫—醫—醫生。我—只—只有說—說—說話時候才！」

(F)

辛浦森喉痛，到他醫生那裏請開藥方。醫生的漂亮護士出來應門。

「醫生在家嗎？」辛浦森沙啞地輕聲問道。

「不在，進來吧！」年青的小姐也輕聲回話說。

(G)

A PATIENT WAS MAKING his first visit to the doctor.

"And whom did you consult❶ about your illness before you came to me?" the doctor inquired.

"Only the druggist❷ down at the corner," replied the patient.

The doctor did not conceal his contempt for the medical advice of people not qualified to practice medicine.

"And what sort of ridiculous advice did that fool give you?"

"He told me," replied the patient innocently, "to see you."

註釋: ❶ consult: 請（醫生）看病
　　　❷ druggist: 藥劑師

◆◆◆◆◆◆◆◆◆◆◆◆◆◆◆◆◆◆◆

(H)

"TELL ME THE TRUTH,"the sick man told his doctor." I want to know just how ill I am."

"Well," said the doctor, "you are very sick-very low. In fact, I feel that I should ask you if there is anyone you would like to see."

"Yes," murmured the patient feebly.

"Who is it?"

"Another doctor."

(G)

一個病人首次去找一個醫生看病。

「在來我這裏之前你是去找那一個看病的？」醫生問道。

「就是角上的那個藥劑師。」病人回答說。

醫生隱藏不住他對於無照醫生所給的醫療建議的輕視。

「那個傻瓜給了你什麼樣的荒謬建議呢？」

「他告訴我，」病人天眞地回答說：「來看你。」

(H)

「告訴我眞話吧！」病人對醫生說：「我想知道我的病到底有多重。」

「噢，」醫生說：「你的病很重─人很虛。事實上我覺得我應該問你有沒有想見（最後一面）的人。」

「有，」病人無力的低聲說。

「是那一個呢？」

「別的醫生。」

15. DRESS

(A)

Moe went to a department store to buy himself a suit. He found just the style he wanted, so he took the jacket off the hanger and tried it on.❶

A salesman came up to him. "Yes, sir. It looks wonderful on you."

"It may *look* wonderful," said Moe irritably, "but it fits terrible. The shoulders pinch."

The salesman didn't bat an eye. "Put on the pants," he suggested. "They'll be so tight, you'll forget all about the shoulders!"

註釋: ❶ try on: 試穿

衣 着

(A)

　　莫到百貨公司去買西裝。他找到一套恰巧是他所要的式樣，便把上衣從架子上拿下來試穿。

　　一個售貨員走過來說：「對了，先生。你穿這件好看極了。」

　　「看起來也許很好，」莫感覺不自在地說：「可是太不合身了。肩膀是繃緊的。」

　　售貨員連眼睛都沒有眨動。「穿上褲子好了，」他建議道：「褲子會緊得讓你整個忘掉肩膀！」

(B)

MRS. ROSENBUSH was negotiating for a mink stole❶ at Mendelovitch's. She asked a lot of questions.

"If I buy the coat and I get caught in the rain," she asked the salesmen, "will it get ruined?"❷

"Look, lady," answered Mendelovitch, "did you ever see a mink carrying an umbrella?"

註釋: ❶ stole: 披肩
     ❷ ruin: 弄壞

(B)

　　羅森布希太太在孟得羅維支店內還價買一條貂皮披肩。她
問了很多問題。

　　「如果我買了披肩遇到下雨，」她問售貨員說：「披肩會不
會壞掉？」

　　「嘿，太太，」孟得羅維支回答說：「你看見過貂打傘嗎？」

(C)

A YOUNG LADY purchased an elegant pair of shoes in the most expensive shoe store in New York. After several days she returned to the store, her feet swollen and calloused,❶ and complained that her new shoes weren't comfortable.

"I just can't walk in these shoes," she groaned.

"Madam," the manager said haughtily, "people who have to walk don't buy shoes in this store!"

註釋: ❶ calloused: 變硬／生繭

(C)

　　一位年輕女士在紐約最貴的一家鞋店買了一雙高貴的皮鞋。過了幾天她回到店裏，脚腫着又生了繭，埋怨她的新鞋不合穿。

　　「我穿這雙鞋簡直不能走路，」她痛苦地說。

　　「太太，」經理趾高氣昂地說：「不得不走路的人是不在本店買鞋的。」

16. DRINK & BARROOMS

AN ELDERLY SCOTSMAN who was carrying a bottle of whiskey on his hip, slipped and fell on a wee patch of ice on the pavement. As he got up he felt something wet trickling❶ down his leg.

"I hope it's blood," he murmured.

註釋: ❶ trickle: 滴

酒 與 酒 吧

　　一個年長的蘇格蘭人腰間帶了一瓶威士忌酒，踏到馬路上一小片冰滑倒了。當他爬起來時他覺得有樣濕濕的東西順着腿滴下來。

　　「我希望是血，」他喃喃地說。

17. EMPLOYMENT OFFICE

(A)

A YOUNG MAN was applying for a job❶ in a big company.

"I'm sorry," said the personnel manager, "but the firm is overstaffed; we have more employees now than we really need."

"That's all right," replied the young man, undiscouraged, "the little bit of work I do wouldn't be noticed."

註釋: ❶ apply for (position): 求（職）

◆◆◆◆◆◆◆◆◆◆◆◆◆◆◆◆◆◆◆◆◆◆◆◆

(B)

A watch factory ran an ad for a precision man. The ad offered $100.00 per week. One guy answered the ad, filled out❶ his application and asked for❷ $200.00 a week.

The superintendent asked, "Have you ever worked in a precision factory before?"

The applicant answered, "No."

"And you have the nerve to❸ ask for $200.00 a week?" bellowed the personnel director.

人　事　室

(A)

　　一個年靑人到一家大公司去謀職。

　　「對不起，」人事經理說：「公司的職員已經超額；　我們現有的員工已經比我們需要的多了。」

　　「沒關係，」年靑人不氣餒地回答：「我做的一點點工作不會有人注意的。」

(B)

　　一家製錶工廠登廣告徵聘一名精密工人，週薪一百元。有個男人去應徵，填寫了申請書，要求週薪兩百元。

　　監工問道：「你以前在精密工廠做過嗎？」

　　申請人答道：「沒有。」
　　「那你還膽敢要兩百元週薪？」人事主管吼道。

"Of course!" said the jerk, "You know the work is much harder if you don't know how to do it."

註釋: ❶ fill out: 填寫

❷ ask for: 要求

❸ have the nerve to: 有□的勇氣

　「當然啦！」那未經世故的人說：「你知道，不會做的工作做起來更難啊。」

18. GOLF

(A)

One man, obviously wealthy, opened the conversation, "I'm looking forward to❶ being at my vacation home again. I can't wait to go golfing. I love golf. Do you play?"

The other man did not want to appear uncivilized, so he said, "Of course. I love to golf also. Why, every afternoon since my retirement I've played."

"Oh, then you must be pretty good!" said the rich man. "I play in the low seventies myself," he added modestly.

"Oh, so do I," said the second man. "Of course, if it gets any colder, I go right back to the hotel!"

註釋: ❶ looking forward to: 期待

(B)

Moore spotted Miller at the clubhouse bar one afternoon and rushed over excitedly. "I've heard about the tragedy you experienced last weekend. It must've been terrible!"

Miller sipped his martini❶ and nodded, lowering his head with the unpleasant memory. "I was playing a two-

高 爾 夫

（A）

　　一個顯然富有的人說：「我希望再到我渡假的別墅去。 我等不及打高爾夫。我好愛高爾夫。你打嗎？」

　　另一個人不願顯得不夠文明， 於是他說道：「當然。 我也愛打高爾夫。噢，我退休以後每天下午都打。」

　　「啊，那你一定打得很不錯了！」富人說道：「我個人打七十幾，」他謙虛的說。

　　「噢，我也是，」第二個人說：「當然， 如果天氣再冷， 我馬上就回旅館去了！」

（B）

　　一天下午摩爾在俱樂部的酒吧遇上米勒，興奮地跑了過去。「我聽到了你上週末碰見的慘事。一定糟透了！」

　　米勒呷了一口馬提尼酒點了點頭， 想到不愉快的事把頭垂了下去。「我正在和老克勞福先生打雙人賽，」他嚴肅地細聲說

some❷ with old Mr. Crawford," he murmured solemnly, "and the poor guy dropped dead on the seventh green."❸

"And I heard you carried him all the way❹ back to the clubhouse," Moore said, admiration gleaming in his eyes. "That was quite a job. Old Crawford must've weighed at least 250 pounds."

"Oh," Miller replied, sipping again, "carrying him wasn't difficult. What tired me was putting him down at every stroke, and then picking him up again."

註釋: ❶ martini: 馬提尼酒（雞尾酒之一種）
　　　 ❷ twosome: 雙人賽
　　　 ❸ green: 果嶺／高爾夫球場
　　　 ❹ all the way: 老遠，一路

◆◆◆◆◆◆◆◆◆◆◆◆◆◆◆◆◆◆◆◆

(C)

TWO GOLFERS❶ were marking time before they could tee off.❷ "I suppose you heard," said one, "that Timothy Brown killed his wife."

"Yes, I heard something about it," responded the other, "but how? how did it happen?"

"Oh, with a golf club."

"Oh, is that so? How many strokes?"

註釋: ❶ golfer: 打高爾夫球的人
　　　 ❷ tee off: 從球座打出球

道:「這可憐的傢伙却在第七洞倒地而亡。」

　　「我聽說你還一路把他搬回俱樂部去,」摩爾眼中閃着讚佩的神情說:「那一定够費勁的。 老克勞福大概至少有兩百五十磅重吧。」

　　「噢,」 米勒又呷了一口酒說:「搬他倒不難。 累人的是每打一桿都得把他放下, 然後再抱起來。」

(C)

　　兩個打高爾夫球的人在開始打球前正在記錄時間。「我想你已經聽到,」一個說:「蒂莫西·布朗殺死了他太太。」

　　「是的, 我聽到了一些,」 另外一個回答說:「不過是怎麼回事？是怎麼樣發生的呢？」

　　「噢, 是用一支高爾夫球桿。」

　　「啊, 是嗎？多少桿呀？」

19. GREED & WEALTH

(A)

ONE MILLIONAIRE was so penurious❶ that he sold his mansion, his grounds, his horses, his boats, his cars, and his other properties, except one piece of land and turned all he owned into gold coins.

On the small plot of land he had left, he found a large tree and dug a hole in the ground to bury his coins. Then he returned to live in a hut he had had built. Daily he came to glimpse his wealth, digging it up to look at it, then returning it to the ground.

But a thief began to follow the miser, and after several weeks, he returned one night and stole all the gold. The next day the newly impoverished man was beside himself; he had lost everything.

Then a friend came by and tried to comfort him. "Do not grieve so much," the friend said. "Take a pile of stones and bury them in the hole. Make believe❷ that the gold is still there. It will do you the same service, for when the gold was there you did not make the slightest use of❸ it."

註釋: ❶ penurious: 吝嗇的
　　　❷ make believe: 假裝
　　　❸ make use of: 使用／利用

貪婪與財富

（A）

　　一個非常吝嗇的百萬富翁，把他的宅邸、土地、馬匹、船、車和其他財產全部賣掉，換成金幣，只留下一小塊土地。

　　在他留下的一小塊土地上，他找到一棵大樹，在下面掘了一個洞，把金幣埋了進去。然後他便回到他命人搭蓋的茅屋去住。每天他都來看他的財富，挖出來過目之後，再放回地下。

　　但是有一個賊開始跟踪這守財奴。過了幾星期，他在一個晚上來把全部金子都偷走了。第二天剛變成窮人的男子大爲冒火；他已經失去了一切。

　　後來有一個朋友路過，想要安慰他。「不要太傷心，」朋友說：「拿一堆石頭埋在洞裏好了。就當作金子還在那裏。這對你會發生同樣的作用，因爲金子在那裏的時候，你一點也沒有用過呀。」

(B)

A businessman had become wealthy through years of working very hard and of driving❶ himself to exhaustion, with never any free moment for a social life. But he claimed he was happy with his money and did not really desire anything else.

One day, however, he realized that money in the bank wasn't enough. What he wanted was land! But land cost too much. He was unwilling to part with enough money to gain what he considered sufficient property.

A colleague, however, told him of a country far away that had *too much* land! There, they were willing to sell land for minimal amounts, and for your money they would give you as much land as you could walk around in a day, said the friend. The businessman decided to take a plane to the foreign country the very next day.

When he arrived in this far-off country, he found that everything his friend had said was true. The chief of the country said the man should lay down his money wherever he liked at dawn, and then walk as far as he wanted until the sun set again. All the land the man encompassed during the day he would then own.

The man was overjoyed, and being an aggressive sort, he pushed himself to go at a fast pace❷ in order to cover a lot of ground. Many times during the day he became fatigued, but he would not allow himself to stop and rest. He pushed onward, greedy for more land.

(B)

　　一個商人苦幹多年，拼命工作耗盡精力而致富，沒有一點空閒作社交活動。不過他表示有了錢就快樂，眞不想要別的東西了。

　　然而有一天，他悟出單把錢存在銀行是不夠的。他要的是土地！可是土地太貴了。他不願割捨足夠買他所需地產的那麼多錢。

　　一個同僚告訴他在某一遙遠的國度裏有太多的土地！朋友說在那裏，他們願意收很少的錢賣地，而且你付了錢他們就會把你一天之內走到的地都給你。商人決定第二天便搭飛機到那異國去。

　　當他抵達那遙遠的國家時，他發現他朋友講的話是眞的。那國的首領說他應該在黎明時把錢放在隨便一處地方，然後願意走多遠就多遠，直到日落爲止。一天之間他所繞過的土地就都屬他所有了。

　　這人大喜，由於他野心勃勃，他勉強快步向前走，以便經過更多的土地。白晝他有很多次疲倦了，但不肯停下來休息。他勉強向前走，貪心想拿到更多土地。

Finally, the sun began to set, and the tribal chief and his men came out in search of the businessman. When they found him, it was just as they'd expected. The man's heart had given out❸ from being pushed so hard. The men dug up six feet of land for him where he lay dead; then they took his money and walked away.

> 註釋: ❶ drive: 拼命做
>
> ❷ at a fast pace: 快步
>
> ❸ give out: 疲倦，疲累

◆◆◆◆◆◆◆◆◆◆◆◆◆◆◆◆◆◆◆

(C)

MANY WEALTHY MEN are known for their penurious habits. It is often said that millionaires make their money by watching every penny.

A cabbie❶ once recognized Nathan Rothschild while driving the financier❷ to his London home. When Rothschild alighted and paid his fare, the driver was disappointed to discover that the tip he received was quite small.

"You know, Mr. Rothschild," he said, "your daughter Julie gives me a much larger tip than that."

"That's all right for her," observed Rothschild dryly. "*She's* got a rich father."

> 註釋: ❶ cabbie: 計程車司機
>
> ❷ financier: 金融家

最後，天漸漸黑了，部落的首領和他的部屬跑出來搜尋那商人。當他們找到那人時，情況正如他們所料一樣。那人的心臟由於過勞而衰竭。部屬們掘了一塊六英尺的土地讓死者睡進去。然後他們就把他的錢拿走了。

(C)

許多富翁因他們吝嗇的習慣而聞名。一般人常說百萬富翁的錢是由注意每一分錢賺來的。

一個計程車司機有一次載奈珊‧羅斯查爾德到他倫敦的寓所時，認出了這位金融家。當羅斯查爾德下車付車資時，司機發現他拿到的小費很少，因而感到失望。

「你知道，羅斯查爾德先生，」他說：「你女兒朱莉給我的小費比這多得多了。」

「她可以那樣，」羅斯查爾德冷冷地說：「她有個濶爸爸。」

20. HAYSEEDS & COUNTRY LIFE

(A)

The Texan visiting Vermont asked a farmer how large his farm was.

"Oh, it's rather large," the Yankee replied, "about 200 yards in that direction and nearly 300 in that."

The Texan chuckled. "Back home in Texas," he said, "Ah❶ have a house at one end of my ranch. Ah can get into my car at the house, step on the gas, and at the end of the day Ah still won't have reached the other end of the ranch."

The Yankee farmer nodded sympathetically. "Yeah, I once had a car like that, too."

註釋: ❶ Ah=I (方言口音)

◆◆◆◆◆◆◆◆◆◆◆◆◆◆◆◆◆◆◆◆◆

(B)

A KENTUCKY MOUNTAINEER❶ wrote to a mail-order❷ house to ask the price of toilet paper. He received a letter directing him to look on page 241 of their catalogue.

"If I had your catalogue," the mountaineer wrote back, "would I need toilet paper?"

註釋: ❶ mountaineer: 山地人
　　　❷ mail-order: 郵購

鄉下人與鄉村生活

(A)

一個德克薩斯佬到佛蒙特去玩，問一個農人他的農場有多大。

「噢，相當大喲，」洋基佬回答說：「往那個方向說大概有兩百碼，往那邊將近三百碼。」

德州佬吃吃地笑了。「在德州家鄉，」他說道：「俺在俺牧場的一頭有棟房子。俺可以在房子的地方坐進車裏，踩動油門，直到晚上還到不了牧場的那一頭。」

洋基農人同情地點點頭。「是啊，我以前也有過一部像這樣的車。」

(B)

一個肯塔基的山地人寫了一封信給一家郵購商店打聽衞生紙的價錢。他接到一封信指點他看那家店舖商品目錄的二百四十一頁。

「如果我有你們的目錄，」山地人寫信過去說：「我還需要衞生紙嗎？」

21. HONESTY

(A)

A farmer was on his way to town when he found a wallet
in the road. Looking through the wallet he found $90, a
name and address, and a paper stating: "If found, please
return this wallet. $10 reward."

The farmer quickly changed routes and brought the
wallet back to its owner. But instead of❶ being grateful,
the owner said, "I see you have already removed the ten
dollars due you for your reward."

The poor man swore that he had not; the owner
insisted that $10 was missing. "There was a hundred dollars
in that wallet!"

So they took their tale to the rabbi, who listened
patiently to the farmer, and then to the owner of the
wallet. "who will you believe, rabbi," ended the rich man,
that ignorant farmer or me?"

"You, of course," answered the rabbi. The farmer was
aghast.

But then the rabbi took the wallet and handed it over
to the farmer. Now it was the owner's turn to be astonished. "What are you doing?" he sputtered.❷

"You said your wallet contained one hundred dollars.
This man says the wallet he found contained only ninety.

誠　　實

（A）

　　一個農人在進城的途中，在路上拾到一個皮夾。打開皮夾，他看到裏面有九十塊錢，另有姓名地址和一張紙條寫着：「如拾到這皮夾，請送還，當酬謝十元。」

　　農人很快就改變路線，把皮夾送還給它主人。然而皮夾的主人非但不感激，反而說道：「我看你是已經把應該給你做酬勞的十塊錢拿掉了。」

　　可憐的農人發誓說沒有拿。皮夾的主人却堅持少了十塊錢。「這皮夾裏原來有一百塊的！」

　　於是他們把這件事告訴了猶太教的牧師。牧師耐心地聽農人講，然後再聽皮夾的主人講。「你相信誰呢，牧師，」富人最後說：「那無知的農人還是我？」

　　「當然是你，」牧師回答說。農人大驚。

　　但是牧師拿起皮夾，把它交給了農人。現在輪到皮夾的主人大吃一驚了。「你做什麼呀？」他急忙說道。

　　「你說你的皮夾裏裝着一百塊錢。這人說他看到的皮夾裏只有九十塊。所以這皮夾不會是你的，」牧師斷然地說。

Therefore, this wallet can't be yours," said the rabbi with finality.

"But what about my lost money?" cried the indignant man.

Patiently, the rabbi explained, "We must wait until someone finds a wallet with one hundred dollars in it."

註釋: ❶ instead of: 代替
　　　❷ sputter: 急忙地講

「那我丟掉的錢怎麼辦呢？」那人憤然叫道。

牧師不慌不忙地解釋說:「我們一定要等到有人找到一個裏面有一百塊錢的皮夾了。」

22. INFIDELITY

(A)

GEORGE'S WIFE WAS becoming suspicious as George's hours became more and more irregular. One night his wife, determined to find out where he'd been spending his time, wired to five of George's friends: "George is not home. Is he spending the night with you?"

By the time George arrived home that night, his wife had received five telegrams all reading: "Yes."

◆◆◆◆◆◆◆◆◆◆◆◆◆◆◆◆◆◆◆

(B)

A HUSBAND COMPLAINED that his wife was a liar. "What makes you say that?" said his friend.

"Well," said the husband, "She came home this morning and told me she spent the night with Eleanor."

"Well," replied the friend, "May be she did. How do you know she's lying?"

"How do I know, because *I* spent the night with Eleanor."

不 忠 誠

(A)

因為喬治的時間變得越來越不規則，他的太太起了疑心。一天夜晚，他太太決定查查看他是在什麼地方消磨他的時間，便打了電報給喬治的五個朋友說：「喬治不在。是否與你共度今夜？」

當晚喬治回家時，他太太接到五個電報都說：「是。」

(B)

一個丈夫埋怨他太太是個說謊的人。

「你為什麼會這樣講？」他的朋友說道。
「噢，」丈夫說：「她今天早上回家，告訴我她昨天和愛麗娜一起過的夜。」
「啊，」朋友回答道：「也許是的。你怎麼知道她說謊呢？」

「我怎麼知道，因為我昨天和愛麗娜一起過夜的。」

23. INSURANCE

(A)

IT WAS BERNIE'S first day as a health-insurance salesman. For his first prospect, he was given the name of the president of a big corporation. If the man bought a policy,❶ Bernie was empowered❷ to speed up proceedings by bringing back a urine sample for processing the same day.

Bernie was gone all morning. When he came back that afternoon, he was carrying the signed policy and a large bucket.

Pleased with himself, Bernie showed his boss the policy. "That's great," the boss smiled. "But what's in the bucket?

"What do you mean 'what's in the bucket'?" Bernie puffed❸ with pride, "I sold the company a group policy!"

> 註釋: ❶ policy: 保險單
> ❷ empower: 授以權力
> ❸ puff: 使自滿

◆◆◆◆◆◆◆◆◆◆◆◆◆◆◆◆◆◆◆◆

(B)

TO INCREASE CIRCULATION, a certain newspaper advertised an accident policy❶ free to all new subscribers. A few days later, this advertisement appeared in the paper:

保　　　險

（A）

　　那是巴尼擔任健康保險經紀人的第一天。他拿到了一家大公司董事長的名字，是他有希望拉到的第一個客戶。公司授權給巴尼，在對方願買保險時，爲了加速辦手續，讓他帶回小便採樣，以備當日處理。

　　巴尼出去了一整個上午。他下午回來時，帶着簽了字的保單和一個大桶。

　　巴尼自覺得意，把保單拿給他老闆看。「那好極了，」老闆笑着說：「桶裏又是什麼呢？」
　　「你問桶裏是什麼是什麼意思？」巴尼自豪地說：「我是賣給了公司一份團體險啊！」

（B）

　　爲了增加銷路，某報刊登廣告說爲每一位新訂戶保了一份免費意外險。幾天後，該報上出現了這樣一則廣告：

"P. J. Melton subscribed to our paper and was given a free accident policy. On his way home from work, he fell down a flight of stairs❷ and broke an arm, a jaw, and both legs. The accident policy paid him $1,000. *You may be the lucky one tomorrow.*"

註釋:　❶ accident policy:　意外保險
　　　　❷ a flight of stairs:　一連的階梯

「庇・傑・梅爾頓訂閱本報，獲得一份免費意外保險。梅君下班返家途中，自階梯摔下，跌傷一臂及下顎與雙腿。意外保險付給他一千元。明天你可能是這位幸運兒。」

24. JAIL

(A)

Frederick II of Prussia, also known as Frederick the Great, instituted social reforms and improvements throughout his country. One day, he unexpectedly visited a prison to inspect the facilities. The head jailer was dismayed to be asked to show the King through the jail itself to see the conditions personally.

As Frederick proceeded through the jail, the convicted men❶ came running up to him, pleading innocence and begging for pardons. The King listened to all, and walked on. He became surrounded by men claiming they were not guilty.

One man, however, stayed in his corner. The King was surprised. "You, there," he called. "Why are you here?"

"Robbery, Your Majesty," stated the prisoner.

"And are you guilty?" asked Frederick.

"Entirely guilty, Your Majesty. I richly deserve my punishment."

The King parted the throng❷ with his walking stick and pointed it at the jailer. "Warden,"❸ he said, "release this guilty wretch at once. I will not have him here in jail where by example he will corrupt all the splendid

監　牢

（A）

　　以弗列德利克大帝聞名的普魯士弗列德利克二世，在他國裏作了一些社會改革和改良措施。有一天，他突然到一座監獄去視察那裡的設備。牢頭被指派隨侍國王巡視監獄，讓國王親自看裡面的情形，心中有些惶恐。

　　當弗列德利克在監獄中走動時，囚犯都跑上來，申訴說自己無罪，並乞求赦免。國王聽了大家說的話，繼續走下去。他漸漸被自稱無罪的人們包圍了。

　　但是有一個人躭在角落裏不動。國王覺得驚訝。「喂, 你,」他叫道:「你為什麼在這裏？」

　　「竊盜, 陛下。」囚犯說道。
　　「那麼你有罪嗎？」弗列德利克問。
　　「完全有罪, 陛下。我是充分應該得到我所受的刑罰。」

　　國王拿着手杖離開人群，並用手杖指了指牢頭。「典獄長,」他說:「立刻放掉這個有罪的傢伙。 我不要讓他在牢裏做樣子把裏面所有無辜的大好人都帶壞了。」

innocent people who occupy it."

　　註釋:　❶ the convicted men: 囚犯
　　　　　❷ throng: 人群
　　　　　❸ warden: 典獄長

◆◆◆◆◆◆◆◆◆◆◆◆◆◆◆◆◆◆◆

(B)

A prisoner in an ancient kingdom was once judged guilty of a crime by his king and sentenced to death. The prisoner begged the king for a reprieve.❶ If his execution were delayed for one year, the prisoner promised to teach the king's horse to fly.

　　Surprised, but too curious not to give it a try, the king agreed, and the prisoner went home. A neighbor came by to congratulate him, but also asked, "Why delay the inevitable?"❷

　　The condemned man explained, "It's not inevitable. The odds❸ are four-to-one in my favor: (1) The king might die. (2) I might die. (3) The horse might die. (4) I might teach the horse to fly."

　　註釋:　❶ reprieve: 緩刑（尤指死刑的）
　　　　　❷ inevitable: 不可避免的
　　　　　❸ odds: 優劣之差／勝算

(B)

　　一個古代王國的犯人因罪被國王判處了死刑。犯人乞求國王緩刑。他說如果能延遲一年執行他的死刑，他一定敎國王的馬飛。

　　國王很驚訝，但又非常好奇，想讓他一試，便答應了。犯人也回了家。一個鄰居跑來向他道賀，但問他說:「不可逃避的事爲什麼要延緩呢？」

　　死刑囚解釋說:「這並不是不可逃避的事。我佔了四對一的有利情勢: 第一，國王也許會死。第二，我也許會死。第三，馬也許會死。第四，我也許敎了馬飛。」

25. LABOR

(A)

A factory in the Northwest operated on a single, huge electrical generator, and the plant fell into❶ complete helplessness on the day the power source broke down. Repairmen tried everything possible, but without success. Finally, since inactivity was an extravagance the factory could not afford, the president sent to the parent company for an expert.

When the man arrived, everyone at the plant crowded around him. The president directed him to the generating room and said, "Jones, I hope you can help us." The man said nothing, but began to slowly examine every pipe, every dial, every switch on the generator.

Finally, Jones stopped in front of a particular pipe and produced a small hammer from his tool kit.❷ His audience watched in awe. Gingerly, he felt with his fingers for the right spot. Then he tapped the hammer carefully at just the right angle. Immediately, the generator began to run again.

The president smiled in relief and said, "Well done,❸ sir! And what is your fee?"

"Five hundred and five dollars," said Jones.

The president was suddenly prudent. "Five hundred

勞　力

(A)

西北部的一家工廠靠一部巨大的發電機運轉，有一天電源損斷，工廠陷入了一籌莫展的情況。修理匠試了一切可試的方法，但無效果。最後，因爲工廠禁不起停工的損失，廠長便要求總公司派一位專家來。

人到時，廠裏所有的人都擁向他身旁。廠長領他到發電室說：「鍾斯，我希望你能幫助我們。」那人沒有講話，只是開始慢慢檢查發電機上的每一條管子、每一個指針盤和開關。

最後鍾斯在一條特別的管子前面停了下來，再從他工具袋裏取出一把小鎚。他的觀衆以敬畏的眼神望着。他小心翼翼地用手指摸索找正確的地方，然後謹愼地用鎚輕輕敲打正確的角度。發電機立刻開始轉動了。

廠長放心地笑着說：「做得好，先生！你的費用是多少呢？」

「五百零五塊。」鍾斯說。

廠長突然精明起來。「單用鎚子敲敲管子就要五百零五塊？」

and five dollars for simply hitting the pipe with a hammer?"

"Ah," explained Jones. "For that, five dollars. For knowing *where* to hit, five hundred dollars."

> 註釋: ❶ fall into: 陷入
> ❷ tool kit: 工具袋
> ❸ well done: 做得好

◆◆◆◆◆◆◆◆◆◆◆◆◆◆◆◆◆◆◆

(B)

A woman was showing a contractor❶ through the second floor of her new house, advising him what colors to paint the rooms. "I'd like the bedroom done in blue", she instructed.

The contractor walked over to the window and shouted: "Green side up! Green side up!"

"I want the bathroom in white!" continued the woman.

Again the contractor yelled out the window, "Green side up! Green side up!"

"The halls should be done in gray!"

Again the contractor shouted out the window, "Green side up! Green side up!"

"Every time I give you a color, you shout 'Green side up!'" the woman snapped❷ angrily.

"I'm sorry, ma'am." the contractor explained. "But I've got three dumb laborers down there below putting in the lawn."

> 註釋: ❶ contractor: 承包人
> ❷ snap: 怒罵／吼着說

「啊，」鍾斯解釋道:「敲敲是五塊錢。知道敲什麼地方，要五百塊。」

(B)

一個婦人正在帶包商看她新房子的二樓，告訴他房間要粉刷什麼顏色。「我想把臥室刷成藍色，」她指示說。

包商走到窗邊叫道:「綠面朝上！綠面朝上！」

「浴室我要白色！」婦人繼續說。

包商又向窗外喊道:「綠面朝上！綠面朝上！」
「過道應該刷灰色！」
包商再度向窗外叫道:「綠面朝上！綠面朝上！」

「每次我告訴你一個顏色，你就叫『綠面朝上！』」婦人生氣地說。
「對不起，太太。」包商解釋道:「只是我有三個笨工人在下面舖草皮呢。」

26. LAWYERS & THE COURT

(**A**)

Clarence Darrow's way with words was not restricted only to the courtroom.

A worried litigant❶ found her troubles were over the minute she retained Darrow; the lawyer defended her brilliantly and won her case hands down.❷

When it was all over, the client said to him, "Oh, Mr. Darrow, how can I ever show my appreciation?"

"My dear woman," Darrow responded with equanimity,❸ "ever since the Phoenicians invented money, there has been only one answer to that question."

註釋: ❶ litigant: 訴訟當事人
　　　❷ hands down: 容易（取勝）
　　　❸ equanimity: 鎮靜

律師與法庭

(**A**)

克拉侖斯·達婁用語的習慣，並不限於在法庭上。

一個心焦的訴訟當事人，在聘請到達婁的一刻，就知道她的麻煩已經消失了。達婁出色地爲她辯護，並輕易地贏了官司。

事過之後，顧客對他說：「哦，達婁先生，我要怎樣才能表示我的謝意呢？」

「太太，」達婁鎮定地回答說：「自從腓尼基人發明了錢以後，對這個問題只有一個答案。」

(B)

AT A MURDER TRIAL, the jury❶ had been debating for sixteen hours. Wearily the jury members returned to the jury box. Just before the verdict was disclosed, the foreman❷ turned to the judge and said, "Your honor, may we ask a question?"

The judge said, "Of course, speak up."

"Well," said the foreman, "Before we pass judgment, we'd like to know if the defendant prefers AC❸ or DC❹ current?"

註釋: ❶ jury: 陪審團
　　　❷ foreman: 陪審長
　　　❸ AC=alternating current: 交流電
　　　❹ DC=direct current: 直流電

◆◆◆◆◆◆◆◆◆◆◆◆◆◆◆◆◆◆◆◆

(C)

Mr. Lavy went to see his lawyer. He was quite distraught.❶ "What am I going to do?" he asked. "Finkel is suing me for breaking an irreplaceable jar of his!"

The lawyer seemed calm. "Don't worry, Mr. Levy," he soothed. "We have at least three lines of defense. In the first place❷, we will prove that you never borrowed the jar from Finkel. In the second place, we'll prove that when you borrowed the jar, it was already damaged beyond❸ repair. And in the third place, we'll prove that when you returned it, it was in absolutely perfect condition."

註釋: ❶ distraught: 煩惱的
　　　❷ in the first (second, third) place: 第一 (二, 三)
　　　❸ beyond: 難於

(B)

　　在一宗謀殺案的審判中，陪審團已經辯論了十六小時。陪審員疲倦地回到陪審團席位。恰恰在宣佈判決之前，陪審長轉向審判官說：「閣下，我們可以問一個問題嗎？」

　　審判官說：「當然，說吧。」

　　「哦，」陪審長說：「在下判決之前，我們想知道被告比較喜歡交流電還是直流電？」

(C)

　　雷維先生去看他的律師。他很煩惱。「我該怎麼辦呢？」他問道：「芬克爾要告我，因為我打破了他一只無法賠還的瓶子。」

　　律師顯得相當鎮定。「不必擔心，雷維先生，」他安慰道：「我們至少有三條線可以抗辯。第一，我們將證明你從未向芬克爾借瓶子。第二，我們將證明你借來的時候，瓶子已經損壞到無法修補的地步。第三，我們將證明你還給他的時候，瓶子絕對是完好無缺的。」

27. LITERARY WORLD

(A)

A delightful children's book, *Dr. Dan the Bandage Man*, was in the works at a publishing house, and the Editor-in-Chief❶ thought of a clever idea. He would include a number of actual Band-Aids in each book.

So he wrote to a friend of his at Johnson and Johnson, manufacturers of Band-Aids, saying, "Please ship two million Band-Aids immediately."

The reply came the next day. "Band-Aids on the way," it said. "What the hell❷ happened to you?"

註釋: ❶ Editor-in-Chief: 總編輯
　　　❷ what the hell: 究竟是

◆◆◆◆◆◆◆◆◆◆◆◆◆◆◆◆◆◆

(B)

ILKA CHASE had recently published her book, *Past Imperfect*, when she encountered❶ a noted Hollywood actress at a party.

"I enjoyed your book," cooed❷ the star saccharinely.❸ "Who wrote it for you?"

文 學 界

（A）

一本名「丹博士和繃帶人」的可愛的童話書，正在出版公司付印。總編輯想到了一個聰明的辦法。他要在每一本書裏附一些真的膠帶。

於是他就寫了一封信給製造膠帶的嬌生公司一個朋友說：「請卽船運二百萬份膠帶。」

第二天回信來了。「膠帶已付運，你究竟出了什麼事？」

（B）

伊爾卡・蔡斯出版了她的書"不完全的過去"。不久，在一次宴會上遇到了一位好萊塢有名的女演員。

「我欣賞了你的書，」明星嗲聲甜甜地說：「是誰替你寫的呢？」

"Darling, I'm so glad you liked it," Ilka replied shrewdly. "Who read it to you?"

註釋: ❶ encounter: 遇見
　　　❷ coo: 唧唧咕咕地講／嗲聲嗲氣地講
　　　❸ saccharinely: 甜蜜地

◆◇◆◇◆◇◆◇◆◇◆◇◆◇◆◇◆◇◆

(C)

HORACE LIVERIGHT, founder of a successful and highly regarded publishing house, was a very busy man and sometimes didn't remember what decision he'd reached in certain projects.

Elliot Paul tells a story of the time he'd submitted his manuscript of *The Governor of Massachusetts* to Liveright, only to have it returned. "Cut 10,000 words," was the note that accompanied the package.

Paul didn't open the package for ten days. Then he sent it back to his publisher, still unopened.

Liveright wrote him by return mail.❶ "Congratulations!" read the letter. "Now it's perfect!"

註釋: ❶ by return mail: 立即託郵作覆

◆◇◆◇◆◇◆◇◆◇◆◇◆◇◆◇◆◇◆

「親愛的，我眞高與你喜歡它，」伊爾卡鋒利地應對道:「是誰讀給你聽的呢？」

(C)

一家發達而受重視的出版公司的創辦人荷列斯・利弗萊特是個大忙人，有時會記不得某些計畫他作了什麼決定。

埃利奧特・波爾講了一個故事，說他有一次把他"麥薩諸賽的州長"一書的原稿交給了利弗萊特，結果被退回。包裹附有一張字條寫着:「刪去一萬字。」

波爾十天沒有打開包裹。然後原封不動又把包裹寄回給他的出版商。

利弗萊特立卽覆了一信。信上說:「恭喜！現在是無懈可擊了。」

(D)

RUDYARD KIPLING once received an unusual letter from some students at Oxford University. Gossip❶ had it that Kipling received a shilling a word for what he wrote. The students enclosed a shilling and requested, "Please send us one of your words."

Kipling's reply was prompt: "Thanks!"

註釋: ❶ gossip: 閒話

◆◆◆◆◆◆◆◆◆◆◆◆◆◆◆◆◆◆◆◆

(E)

LATE IN LIFE, prolific❶ author W. Somerset Maugham came to the United States. While the author visited a university one day, a young man came to him and asked for Maugham's help. He'd just written a novel and wanted Maugham to give him a good title for it. Would the famous writer read through the manuscript?❷

Maugham's reply was prompt. "There is no necessity for reading your book," said he. "Are there any drums in it?"

"No," stated the young man, "it's not that kind of a story. You see, it deals with......"

Maugham held up his hand and went on. "Are there any bugles in it?" he asked.

"No," said the young author, now puzzled.

(D)

魯得亞・基普林有一次收到牛津大學學生寄來一封奇特的信。傳說基普林寫的文章一個字收一先令。學生們附了一先令並要求道:「請寄下您的一個字。」

基普林的答覆迅速:「謝！」

(E)

多產作家森瑪塞・毛姆晚年來到美國。當這位作家有一天去訪問一所大學時, 一個學生跑來請求他幫助。學生寫了一篇小說, 想請毛姆題一個好書名。這位名作家願意閱讀書稿嗎？

毛姆的答覆迅速。「沒有必要看你的書, 」他說:「裏面有鼓嗎？」

「沒有, 」年輕人說:「不是那一類的故事。 你知道, 是關於……」

毛姆擧起手來繼續說下去:「裏面有喇叭嗎？」他問道。

「沒有, 」年輕作家這時迷惑地說。

"Well, then," smiled Maugham, "call it, *No Drums, No Bugles.*"

註釋:　❶ prolific: 多產的／豐富的
　　　　❷ manuscript: 原稿

「那，好吧！」毛姆笑了，「就叫『無鼓，無喇叭』好了。」

28. MARITAL LIFE

(A)

"My wife," said Koblinsky, "is so educated, so well read, that she can talk for hours and hours on any subject you name."

"Huh," scoffed❶ Michaelson, "that's nothing. My wife can talk for hours and hours and doesn't even require a subject."

　　註釋: ❶ scoff: 嘲笑

❖❖❖❖❖❖❖❖❖❖❖❖❖❖❖❖❖❖❖

(B)

Often the only one able to get the better of❶ a wit is his wife. Mrs. George Bernard Shaw listened one day to her husband's clever logic promoting men as wiser than women.

"Of course, you're right, my dear," responded Mrs. Shaw placidly. "After all,❷ you married me and I you."

　　註釋: ❶ get the better of: 超過／勝過
　　　　　❷ after all: 畢竟／到底

❖❖❖❖❖❖❖❖❖❖❖❖❖❖❖❖❖❖❖

婚 姻 生 活

（A）

「我的太太，」柯布林斯基說：「教育程度眞好，書也看得眞多，無論你說什麽話題，她都能一聊聊上好幾個鐘頭。」

「呵，」麥克爾遜嘲笑着說：「那不算什麽。我太太可以一講講上好幾個鐘頭，並不需要話題。」

（B）

唯一能勝過一個人的機智的，往往是他太太。有一天喬治・蕭伯納太太聽到她丈夫在鼓勵男人比女人聰明的理論。

「當然你是對的，親愛的，」蕭太太沈着地回答：「反正你娶了我，我嫁了你。」

(C)

IT WAS A FEARFUL NIGHT. Lightning shot through the sky and the thunder roared in blasts that would frighten anybody. The rain came down in sheets.❶

The door of a little bakery opened and a drenched man came up to the counter and said, "Let me have two bagels."❷

The baker looked at him incredulously. "What," said the baker, "you came out on a night like this just for two bagels? That's all?"

"Yes, that's all," answered the man. "That's all I need. Just one for me and one for Pauline."

"Who's Pauline?" asked the baker.

"Oh what the hell difference is it to you?" answered the man. "Pauline is my wife. Who do you think she is? Would my mother send me out on a night like this?"

> 註釋:　❶ in sheets: 傾盆地下
> 　　　 ❷ bagel: 圓圓圈形的麵包

❖❖❖❖❖❖❖❖❖❖❖❖❖❖❖❖❖

(D)

PORTER PACED BACK and forth in the doctor's waiting room while his wife underwent a complete physical examination inside. Finally the doctor opened the door and summoned the husband. "To be blunt,❶ Mr. Porter," he said gravely, "I don't like the looks of your wife."

(C)

那是一個可怕的夜晚。天空閃着閃電，雷聲隆隆地響着，什麼人都會害怕。雨也傾盆似的降下來。

一家小麵包店的門打開了。一個淋得濕透的男人走近櫃臺說：「給我兩個圓麵包。」

賣麵包的用懷疑的眼神望望他說：「什麼，你在這樣的一個晚上跑出來，只為兩個圓麵包？就只有這一點嗎？」

「是啊，只有這點，」那人回答說：「我只需要這些。我一個，保琳一個。」

「保琳是誰啊？」賣麵包的問。

「這到底跟你有什麼關係？」那人回答說：「保琳是我太太。你以為她是誰？我媽會在這樣一個晚上差我出來嗎？」

(D)

波特在她太太接受徹底的身體檢查時，在醫生的候診室裏來回地踱着。最後醫生打開門把這位丈夫叫了進去。「波特先生，」他嚴肅地說：「坦率地講，我不喜歡你太太的樣子。」

"Neither do I," Porter responded, "but she's great with the kids."

註釋: ❶ blunt: 直率的

◆◆◆◆◆◆◆◆◆◆◆◆◆◆◆◆◆◆◆◆

(E)

THE NEW NEIGHBOR joined the mah johngg❶ group for the first time, and all the ladies gaped at the huge diamond she wore.

"It's the third most famous diamond in the world," she told the women confidentially. "First is the Hope diamond, then the Kohinoor diamond, and then this one—the Rabinowitz diamond."

"It's beautiful!" admired one woman enviously. "You're so lucky!"

"Not so lucky," the newcomer maintained. "Unfortunately, with the famous Rabinowitz diamond, I have received the famous Rabinowitz curse."❷

"And what is that?" wondered the women.

The woman heaved an enormous sigh. "Mr. Rabinowitz," she said.

註釋: ❶ mahjohngg: 麻將牌
      ❷ curse: 詛咒／災禍

◆◆◆◆◆◆◆◆◆◆◆◆◆◆◆◆◆◆◆◆

「我也不喜歡,」波特回答說:「可是她對孩子們好極了。」

(E)

新來的鄰居第一次參加痲將會，所有的女士看到她佩戴的鑽石都目瞪口呆。

「這是全世界第三顆最有名的鑽石,」她坦白地告訴那些女太太們說:「第一是希望鑽石，然後是柯希奴鑽石，再下來就是這一顆——拉比諾維玆鑽石了。」

「好漂亮！」一位女士羨慕地讚美道:「你眞幸運！」

「不那麼幸運,」新來者表示意見說:「不幸的是，我得到了有名的拉比諾維玆鑽石，同時也得到了有名的拉比諾維玆禍害。」

「那是什麼？」女太太們懷疑地問。

她嘆了一大口氣說:「拉比諾維玆先生。」

(F)

THE HUSBAND CAME HOME drunk again. His wife couldn't stand it. She screamed at him, "If you don't stop this damnable drinking, I'm going to kill myself."

The hapless❶ husband retorted,❷ "Promises, that's all I get. Promises."

註釋: ❶ hapless: 倒霉的／不幸的
　　　❷ retort: 回嘴

◆◇◆◇◆◇◆◇◆◇◆◇◆◇◆◇◆◇◆◇◆◇◆

(G)

TWO WOMEN MET again after many years and began exchanging histories. "Whatever happened to your son?" asked one woman.

"Oh, what a tragedy!"❶ moaned❷ the other. "My son married a no-good who doesn't lift a finger around the house. She can't cook, she can't sew a button on a shirt, all she does is sleep. My poor boy brings her breakfast in bed, and all day long she stays there, loafing, reading, eating candy!"

"That's terrible," sympathized the first woman. "And what about your daughter?"

"Oh, she's got a good life. She married a man who's a living doll! He won't let her set foot in the kitchen. He gives her breakfast in bed, and makes her stay there all day, resting, reading, and eating chocolates."

註釋: ❶ tragedy: 悲劇
　　　❷ moan: 悲嘆／抱怨

(F)

丈夫又一次喝醉酒回家。 太太不能忍受， 對着他叫喊：
「你要是不停止可惡的喝酒， 我就自殺。」

倒霉的丈夫回嘴說：「許諾， 我得到的只有這些。 空的許
諾。」

(G)

兩個女人多年後再會面， 開始輪流叙述彼此的經歷。「你
兒子怎樣了？」一個女人問。

「唉， 簡直是個悲劇！」另一個女人慨嘆着說：「我兒子娶
了個一無可取的女人， 她在家連抬一抬手指的事都不做。 她不
會燒菜， 不會釘一粒襯衫鈕扣， 只會睡覺。我那可憐的孩子把
她的早餐送到床上， 她却整天躭在那兒， 閒着， 看書， 吃糖
果！」

「眞太糟了，」第一個女人同情地說：「你的女兒怎樣呢？」

「噢， 她日子過得很好。 她嫁了一個像活娃娃似的男人！
他不讓她進厨房。在床上給她吃早餐， 讓她整天躭在那兒， 休
息， 看書， 吃巧克力。」

(H)

Mrs. Meyerowitz met Mrs. Goldstein for a cup of tea one afternoon.

"Did you hear that the Martinsons' stove exploded last night?" began Mrs. Meyerowitz. "Mr. and Mrs. Martinson were blown right out the front door and into the street!"

"If that's true," quipped❶ Mrs. Goldstein, "that's the first time they've gone out together in thirty years."

註釋: ❶ quip: 說諷刺話／嘲弄

◆◇◆◇◆◇◆◇◆◇◆◇◆◇◆◇◆◇◆◇◆

(I)

EVERYONE ACKNOWLEDGED that the Jacobys were the happiest family in the neighborhood. They never quarreled about anything and always seemed to get along.❶ One day, at a cocktail party, the neighbors and friends gathered around Jacoby and asked him how he could account for❷ the marvelous success of his marriage.

"Oh," he said proudly, "Sadie and I made an agreement when we got married. She would make all the small decisions and I would make all the big decisions. And we've kept to that policy through all the years of our marriage."

"Like what kind of big and small decisions?" asked the curious audience.

(H)

一天下午梅耶維支太太和哥爾斯坦太太會面一同喝茶。

「你有沒有聽說馬丁生家的爐子昨天夜裏爆炸了？」梅耶維支太太開始說：「馬丁生先生和太太從前門一起被炸出到馬路上！」

「如果那是眞的，」哥爾斯坦太太諷刺道：「就是他們兩個在三十年裏第一次一起出門。」

(I)

人人都認爲賈柯比是鄰居中最幸福的一家。他們一對從不爲任何事吵架，好像永遠和好相處。一天在雞尾酒會上，鄰居和朋友聚在賈柯比的周圍，問他怎樣使他的婚姻成功得令人驚奇。

「噢，」他得意地說：「莎廸和我結婚的時候曾經有個約定。她決定一切小事我決定一切大事。結婚這些年我們一直遵守這個原則。」

「譬如決定什麼樣的大事和小事呢？」聽的人好奇地問。

"Well," explained Jacoby, "she makes the small decisions like who my son Milton is going to marry; who my daughter Jeanette should go out with; where we should go on our summer vacation; and how much we should spend, for example, on a bar mitzvah❸ present for Tom Seltzer's son; how much we should pay for the maid. That kind of thing, you know."

"And the big decisions?" pursued the crowd.

"Oh," said Jacoby modestly, "I make the fundamental decisions. I decide whether the United States should resume relations with China. I decide how much money Congress should approve for Israel. And I decide who would be the best candidate for president."

註釋: ❶ get along: 和好相處
　　　 ❷ account for: 成為──的理由
　　　 ❸ bar mitzvah: 成年祝典（少年到十三歲時的）

◆◆◆◆◆◆◆◆◆◆◆◆◆◆◆◆◆◆◆◆

(J)

POOR MRS. EISENBERG was beside herself. Her husband had left her, and her daughter Sally was thirty-two years old and still unmarried. She thought about it and worried about it and finally decided to take some action.❶

"Sally," she said, "I think you ought to put an advertisement❷ in the paper." Sally was aghast at the thought.

「啊,」賈柯比解釋道:「她決定小事就像我的兒子米爾頓要娶誰啦;我的女兒賈奈特應該和誰交朋友啦;暑假我們應該到哪裏去啦;我們應該花多少錢啦;譬如送湯姆塞爾則兒子成年儀典的禮物啦;應該付給女佣人多少錢啦。就像這一類的事,你們知道吧。」

「那大事的決定呢?」一群人追問道。

「噢,」賈柯比謙虛的說:「我決定基本上的事。我決定美國是不是應該和中國恢復邦交。我決定國會應該核准多少錢給以色列。我還決定誰是最好的總統候選人。」

(J)

艾森伯太太變得失魂落魄。她丈夫離她而去,女兒莎麗已經三十二歲尚未結婚。她想到這件事就煩惱,最後決定採取一些行動。

「莎麗,」她說:「我想你應該在報上登個廣告。」莎麗對這個想法大爲吃驚。

"No, listen," said Mrs. Eisenberg, "it sounds wild, but I think we should try it. You don't put your name in, just a box number. Here, I wrote one up already." And she showed Sally an ad she had devised:

Charming Jewish Girl, Well-Educated, Fine Cook, Would like to Meet Kind, Intelligent, Educated, Jewish Gentleman. Object: Matrimony.

Sally was embarrassed, but she couldn't talk her mother out❸ of it. So into the paper the ad went. And Sally went every day to see if there were any replies.

A few days later, there was a letter for her. Sally ran home to her mother flushed with excitement. "Look!"she cried.

"Well, hurry up and open it!" urged Mrs. Eisenberg. So Sally tore open the envelope and unfolded the letter. Then she began to cry.

"What's the matter?" asked Mrs. Eisenberg.

Sally's sobs got even louder. "It's from papa!"

註釋: ❶ take action: 採取行動
　　　❷ put advertisement: 登廣告
　　　❸ talk (a person) out of: 說服 (某人) 不做

◆◆◆◆◆◆◆◆◆◆◆◆◆◆◆◆◆◆◆

(K)

MR. AND MRS. MANDELBAUM decided the only solution to their marital problems was in divorce.❶ So they went to see the rabbi.

「不，聽着，」艾森伯太太說：「這好像是離譜，但我想我們應該試試看。你不要出名，只寫郵箱號碼。看，我已經寫好了一個。」於是她把她擬妥的廣告拿給莎麗看。

秀麗猶太少女，曾受良好教育，善烹飪，願會晤親切、聰明而受過教育的猶太男士。目的：結婚。

莎麗有些窘，但她無法說服她媽媽不要這樣做。於是廣告在報上登了出來。莎麗每天去看有無回音。

兩三天後，有了一封給她的信。莎麗跑回家找媽媽，興奮得臉都紅了。「看呀！」她叫喊着。

「啊，趕快拆開！」艾森伯太太催促着。莎麗於是撕開信封，把信拿出來看。然後她就哭起來了。

「怎麼啦？」艾森伯太太問道。

莎麗嗚咽的聲音更大了。「是爸爸寫來的！」

(K)

曼德爾包姆先生和太太決定只有離婚才能解決他們的婚姻問題。於是他們就跑去見猶太教會的長老。

The rabbi was concerned about the three children and was reluctant❷ to see the family broken up. He thought that if he could stall the couple maybe they would work it out together.

"Well," said the rabbi, "there's no way of dividing three children. What you'll have to do is live together one more year. You'll have a fourth child, and then, it will be easy to arrange a proper divorce. You'll take two children, and he'll take two."

"Nothing doing,"❸ said Mrs. Mandelbaum. "Rabbi, if I depended on him, I wouldn't even have had these three!"

註釋: ❶ divorce: 離婚
　　　❷ reluctant: 不情願的
　　　❸ nothing doing: 不行

◆◇◆◇◆◇◆◇◆◇◆◇◆◇◆◇◆◇◆◇◆◇◆◇◆

(L)

HYDE'S WIFE WAS a constant nag,❶ forever comparing her husband to his more affluent❷ friends. "The Marshalls have a new car and the Murrays just bought a new house," she complained. "All our friends live ten times better than we do. If we don't move into a more expensive apartment they'll all be laughing at us!"

長老顧慮三個孩子，不願見到這個家破碎。他想如果他能使這對夫婦左右為難，也許他們會一起設法解決難題。

「啊，」長老說：「沒有辦法分三個孩子呀。你們必須再同居一年。你們會有第四個孩子。到那時就容易安排正式的離婚了。你帶兩個，他帶兩個。」

「不行，」曼德爾包姆太太說：「長老，如果我靠他的話，連這三個都不會有了！」

(L)

海德的太太是個不停嘮叨的女人，總是拿她丈夫和他富有的朋友來比較。「馬歇爾夫婦有了一輛新車，茂雷夫婦剛買了一棟新房子，」她埋怨道：「我們所有的朋友都過得比我們好十倍。如果我們不搬到一個更貴的公寓裏去，他們大家都會笑我們了。」

One night her beleaguered❸ husband came home and told her, "Well, we'll soon be living in a more expensive apartment. The landlord just doubled our rent."

註釋：❶ nag: 愛嘮叨的女人
　　　❷ affluent: 富裕的／富足的
　　　❸ beleaguer: 圍攻

◆◆◆◆◆◆◆◆◆◆◆◆◆◆◆◆◆◆

(M)

"BUT DARLING," the henpecked❶ husband protested,❷ "I'm doing everything I can to make you happy!"

"You don't do one thing my first husband did to make me happy!" she pouted.❸

"And what's that?" the harassed husband asked.

"He died!"

註釋：❶ henpecked: 懼內的／怕老婆的
　　　❷ protest: 反駁
　　　❸ pout: 繃臉／鬧彆扭

◆◆◆◆◆◆◆◆◆◆◆◆◆◆◆◆◆◆

(N)

YONKEL AND FLORRIE were invited to a dinner party at Yonkel's boss's home on Long Island. Yonkel knew he had to go, but he was afraid the people there would be much smarter than he. So he instructed Florrie to keep her mouth shut and not to say anything if she could help it. If someone asked her a direct question, she was to

一天夜晚，她那受攻擊的丈夫回家來告訴她：「好了，我們不久就要住更貴的公寓了。房東剛把我們的租金加了一倍。」

(M)

「可是親愛的，」懼內的丈夫反駁說：「我在盡一切可能使你快活啊！」

「有一件事，我第一個丈夫做了讓我快活的，你沒有做！」她板起臉。

「是什麼事呢？」丈夫困惑地問道。

「他死了！」

(N)

容克爾和佛洛麗接受邀請，到容克爾老闆長島的住宅去晚餐。容克爾知道他不得不去，但他怕那裏的人比他精明得多。因此他關照佛洛麗保持沈默，耐得住的話什麼都不要說。假如有人問她直接的問題，就回答一個是或不是。

answer with just a yes or a no.

Florrie agreed, and the two set off❶ nervously for the party. Yonkel said hardlly a word the whole evening, and Florrie said nothing at all. But this state of affairs began to upset the hostess, who thought that it was her job to draw her guests into the conversation.

So the boss's wife turned to Florrie and said to her kindly, "Tell me, are you acquainted with Beethoven?"

Florrie had been silent for so long, she became flustered at being addressed directly. She stammered and fell all over herself❷ and finally said, "Oh, yes, I met him just the other day on the A train to Coney Island."

The hostess and all the guests were mortified; it took them a few minutes to regain their composure. But eventually, the hostess found her tongue❸ again and smoothed❹ things over by chattering with her other guests.

After all the good-byes were said and Florrie was in the car with Yonkel, the husband lashed out at her. "I thought I told you to keep quiet!" he shouted. "You embarrassed me beyond belief, I hope you know that."

Florrie was crestfallen. Yonkel continued. "My God," he ranted, "There wasn't a single person there who didn't know that the A train does not go to Coney Island!"

註釋: ❶ set off: 出發
　　　❷ fall over oneself: 表現過分熱心
　　　❸ find one's tongue: (嚇了以後) 能開口
　　　❹ smooth over: 彌補／掩飾

　　佛洛麗同意了，兩人便儒怯地出發去赴會。那一晚容克爾幾乎一言未發，佛洛麗更是什麼也沒說。但是這種事態讓女主人感覺不安起來，她想她應該把客人引到會話中去。

　　於是老闆的太太便轉向佛洛麗，親切對她說道：「告訴我，你對貝多芬熟悉吧？」

　　佛洛麗已經沈默了很久。有人直接問話，她驚慌起來。口結了一下，最後拼命說道：「噢，是啊，前幾天我剛剛在去哥尼島的甲號火車上遇見他。」

　　全體客人都為此感到難為情；幾分鐘後他們才恢復冷靜。最後女主人又能開口，藉着和其他客人交談，把事情舖平。

　　大家道別後，佛洛麗和容克爾一起坐上車時，丈夫痛責了她一頓。「我想我告訴過你不要說話！」他大聲喊道：「你讓我丟盡了臉，我希望你知道。」

　　佛洛麗十分沮喪。容克爾繼續往下說：「天啊，」他叫道：「沒有一個人不知道甲號火車是不去哥尼島的！」

(O)

The Marriage Counselor was advising the bride to be. "The first thing I must tell you is that if you want to retain❶ the interest of your husband you must never completely disrobe❷ in front of him when retiring. Always keep a little mystery about you."

About two months later, the husband said to his bride, "Tell me, Jane, is there any insanity❸ in your family?"

"Of course not," she responded hotly. "Why do you ask such a question?"

"Well," said he, "I was merely wondering why, during the last two months since we're married, when you go to bed you never take off your hat."

註釋: ❶ retain: 保持
　　　 ❷ disrobe: 卸裝／脫去衣服
　　　 ❸ insanity: 精神異狀，瘋狂

(O)

婚姻顧問正在替準新娘提供意見。「第一件事我必須告訴你的，就是如果你想保持你丈夫的興趣，就寢時便絕對不要在他面前完全卸裝。永遠要在你身邊保有一點神秘。」

大約兩個月後，丈夫對他的新娘說：「珍，告訴我，你家人裏有沒有神經不正常的？」

「當然沒有，」她激動地回答：「你爲什麼要問這樣的問題？」

「噢，」他說：「我只是覺得奇怪，爲什麼我們結婚兩個月以來，你睡覺的時候總是不脫帽子。」

29. MATCHMAKERS

(A)

A MATCHMAKER❶ TOOK a well-to-do❷ man to meet a prospective bride and her family. While they were waiting in the living room, the matchmaker pointed to the elegance of the surroundings.

"These people are well off.❸ Look at this fine furniture. Take a look at the delicate dishware.❹ Notice the paintings on the wall and the sculpture on the mantel."❺

The businessman was suspicious. "To make a good impression on me, perhaps they have borrowed these things."

At that, the matchmaker scoffed, "Borrowed? Don't be foolish! Who would lend anything to such paupers?"

註釋: ❶ matchmaker: 媒人
　　　❷ well-to-do: 富裕的／小康的
　　　❸ well off: 富裕的
　　　❹ dishware: 餐具
　　　❺ mantel: 壁爐架

◆◆◆◆◆◆◆◆◆◆◆◆◆◆◆◆◆◆◆

(B)

A matchmaker was exulting over the virtues of a particular girl. "She is beautiful, tall, well-built, a good cook, a smart woman, with integrity,"❶ she listed.

媒　　人

(A)

　　一個媒人帶一位富裕的男士會見可能做他新娘的女孩和她的家人。 在客廳等候時， 媒人指着高雅的環境說:「這些人是有錢。看這考究的家具。看看精緻的餐具。注意牆上的畫還有壁爐架上的彫刻。」

　　商人有些懷疑。「也許他們借了這些東西來， 想給我一個好印象。」

　　媒人聽了這話， 便嘲笑說:「借？別傻了！誰會借東西給這種窮光蛋？」

(B)

　　一個媒人與高采烈地在講某一位女士的優點。「她漂亮、高大、身材好、菜燒得好，是個聰明人， 還正直可靠。」 她列舉道。

But the client said, "But you left out❷ one important thing, didn't you?"

"Not possible!" said the matchmaker. "What could I have left out?"

"That she limps!"❸ said the young man.

"Oh!" came the answer, "But only when she walks!"

註釋：　❶ integrity: 誠實／正直

　　　　❷ leave out: 省略／遺漏

　　　　❸ limp: 跛行

◆◆◆◆◆◆◆◆◆◆◆◆◆◆◆◆◆◆◆◆◆◆

(C)

IN A LITTLE TOWN in Russia, there were many more girls than boys. Consequently, the local matchmaker was having an easy time making good matches for the young men of the village, although the girls were often ending up❶ with the poor end of the bargain.

A rather unpleasant man in the village, whose face matched his disposition, wanted a bride who possessed beauty, charm, and talent.

"I have just the girl for you," said the matchmaker. "Her father is rich, and she is beautiful, well-educated, charming. There is only one problem."

"And what is that?" asked the young man, suspiciously.

"She has an affliction.❷ Once a year, this beautiful girl goes crazy. Not permanently, you understand. It's just

但顧客說:「可是你漏了一件重要的事，對吧？」

「不可能啊！」媒人說:「我會漏了什麼呢？」

「她跛脚！」年輕人說。
「噢！」答話來了，「可是那只是在她走路的時候啊！」

(C)

在俄國一個小城裏，女孩比男孩多得多。因此，當地的媒人就不費力地爲村子裏的年青人做成好媒，然而女孩最後便常常在談條件上吃虧。

村子裏有一個討人厭的男人，面貌和性情相稱，想找一個擁有美貌魅力和才智的新娘。

「我剛好有個你要的女孩，」媒人說:「她爸爸有錢，她長得美，受過好敎育，又可愛。只有一個問題。」

「那是什麼？」年青人狐疑地問。
「她有一件苦惱事。一年一次，這位美麗的小姐會發瘋。並不是長期的，你懂得吧。只有一天的工夫，而且她不會惹麻

for one day, and she does not cause any trouble. Then afterwards, she's as charming as ever for another year."

The young suitor considered. "That's not so bad," he decided. "If she's as rich and beautiful as you say, let's go to see her."

"Oh, not now," cautioned the matchmaker. "You'll have to wait to ask her to marry you."

"Wait for what?" pursued the greedy man.

"Wait for the day she goes crazy!" came back the answer.

註釋: ❶ end up: 完結／完畢
　　　❷ affliction: 苦惱

煩。過了以後，在一年間她就和平時一樣可愛了。」

　　年青的求婚者考慮了一下。「那並不太糟，」他決定了。「如果她是像你說的那樣又有錢又美麗，就讓我們去見見她吧。」

　　「啊，現在不行，」媒人告誡說：「你要向她求婚還得等。」

　　「等什麼呢？」貪心的人問。
　　「等她發瘋的那一天！」答案回來了。

30. MILITARY LIFE

(A)

A BRITISH navy admiral tells of the time his fleet was only fifteen minutes into practicing war maneuvers❶ when one particularly inept❷ lieutenant collided❸ his ship with the admiral's.

The admiral knew it was the lietuenant's first command and that the young man was nervous; still, this was a serious error. He wired the lieutenant angrily, "What do you propose to do now?"

Meekly came the return signal, "Buy a small farm, sir."

> 註釋: ❶ maneuvers: 演習
> ❷ inept: 笨拙的／無能的
> ❸ collide with: 碰撞

(B)

In 1948, when Israel declared its independence, Velvil Pasternak flew at once from New York City to offer his services to the fledgling❶ state. He applied at the recruiting❷ office to join the beleaguered Israeli Army.

軍 中 生 活

(A)

　　一位英國海軍上將講他的艦隊有一次作軍事演習，剛開始十五分鐘，一個特別笨拙的上尉便將他的艦撞到上將的艦上去了。

　　上將知道這是上尉初次指揮，而這年青人是緊張了些。不過這仍然是一項嚴重的錯誤。他忿怒地發電給上尉說：「現在你計畫如何？」

　　溫順的回電來了，「買一個小農場，長官。」

(B)

　　當以色列在一九四八年宣告獨立時，魏維爾·巴斯特納克立卽從紐約市飛去，對生齊羽毛的國家提供服務。他到招募新兵處報名，想加入被圍攻的以色列陸軍。

After the usual forms were completed, he was told to go down to Section 1 and pick up his Army gear.❸ He came to the first window and the clerk asked him what size shoes he needed.

"Size 8-1/2," answered Velvil.

The clerk looked around in the stockroom, came back and said, "I'm sorry, we don't have 8-1/2. We're very short of shoes. We got size 8 and we got size 9, but no 8-1/2's."

Velvil hesitated, but the clerk advised, "Look, what do you need shoes for? You got sneakers❹ on. It's perfectly okay. Better than to have shoes that are too small or too big. Forget about shoes. Wear your own sneakers."

Velvil agreed and went to the next window, where he requested a medium-size army shirt. The clerk looked around and came back. "Look, we got size small army shirt and size extra large. Medium we ain't got." Then he looked at Velvil and said, "Look, that shirt that you've got on. That's pretty good. What do you need an army shirt for? Use what you've got."

Velvil agreed and moved on. He went through this at each commissary❺ window and came out with his original set of clothes.

He was then ushered into the medical office. The doctor examined him and asked a few standard questions. "Do you swim?" he asked.

　　填完一般表格後，有人叫他到第一組去領軍服。他到第一個窗口，職員問他需要幾號的皮靴。

　　「八號半。」魏維爾回答。

　　職員在庫房裏周圍看了一下回來說：「對不起，我們沒有八號半的。我們很缺皮靴。有八號和九號的，但沒有八號半的。」

　　魏維爾躊躇了一下。職員建議道：「看，你要皮靴做什麼？你穿着運動鞋，這就完全沒問題啦。比穿太小或太大的皮靴好啊。忘掉皮靴，穿你自己的運動鞋好了。」

　　魏維爾表示同意，走到下一個窗口，請發一件軍服的襯衫。職員四面看了一下回來了。「喂！我們有小號的軍服襯衫和特大號的，中號我們沒有。」然後他望望魏維爾說：「看，你穿的那件襯衫，那很好嘛。你還要軍服襯衫做什麼？就用你有的好了。」

　　魏維爾同意後再向前走去。他到每一個供應處窗口都經過這樣的情形，出來還是穿着他原來的一套衣服。

　　然後有人指引他去醫務室。醫生爲他檢查，並問了幾個例行的問題。「你游泳嗎？」他問。

"What?" exclaimed Velvil. "Ships you ain't got neither?"

註釋:　❶ fledge:　生齊羽毛
　　　　❷ recruit:　徵募（新兵、新會員）
　　　　❸ gear:　衣服
　　　　❹ sneakers:　運動鞋（橡膠底的）
　　　　❺ commissary:　物資供應所

◆◈◆◈◆◈◆◈◆◈◆◈◆◈◆◈◆◈◆◈◆

(C)

AT AN ARMY WELCOMING PARTY, the long-winded❶ commanding general of the base was delivering a boring, self-congratulatory oration. A young second lieutenant, tired of standing, muttered❷ to the woman at his side, "What a pompous❸ old windbag❹ that fool is."

The woman turned to him at once and barked, "Lieutenant, do you know who I am?"

"No, I don't, Ma'am."

"I am the *wife* of that 'pompous old windbag,' as you call him."

"Oh my!" the young lieutenant blanched. "Do you know who I am?"

"No, I don't," said the general's wife.

"Thank God!" the lieutenant replied, slipping off into the crowd.

註釋:　❶ long-winded:　冗長的／囉嗦的
　　　　❷ mutter:　低語
　　　　❸ pompous:　自大的
　　　　❹ windbag:　饒舌的人

「什麼？」魏維爾叫道：「船你們也沒有啊？」

(C)

在一次陸軍的歡迎會上，囉嗦的基地指揮官正在發表一篇令人厭煩的自我標榜的演說。一個年青少尉，站厭了，低聲向他身旁的女人說：「那個笨蛋是個多自大的老饒舌啊。」

女人立刻轉向他大聲吼道：「少尉，你知道我是誰嗎？」

「不，我不知道，太太。」
「我就是你所說那個自大的老饒舌的太太。」

「啊唷！」年青的少尉臉色蒼白。「你知道我是誰嗎？」

「不，我不知道！」將軍的太太說。
「感謝上帝！」少尉回着話，便溜進了人群。

(D)

A TOUGH TOP sergeant glared❶ at the pint-sized❷ rookie❸ and shouted, "What's the first thing you do when you clean a rifle?"

The rookie replied in a low-pitched❹ voice, "Look at the serial number."

"The serial number!" roared the sergeant, "Why look at the serial number?"

"To make sure," explained the rookie mildly, "that I'm cleaning my own rifle."

註釋: ❶ glare (at): 瞪視
　　　❷ pint-size: 小
　　　❸ rookie: 新兵／新參加者
　　　❹ low-pitched: 低調的

❖❖❖❖❖❖❖❖❖❖❖❖❖❖❖❖❖❖

(E)

The United States has been called a melting pot,❶ and this characteristic is never more clearly seen than in war-time. Americans of all national origins rushed to join the army to serve their country during the Second World War.

One forty-year-old Irishman appeared before an enlist-ment officer. The Irishman was anxious to sign up.❷ Husky,❸ strong, and in excellent health, the man would make a fine recruit, but the rules stated a top limit of thirty-eight years of age for enlisting soldiers. The eager patriot was crushed.

(D)

　　一個健壯的上士瞪着矮小的新兵吼道:「你擦來福槍時第一件事做什麽?」

　　新兵低聲答道:「看編號。」

　　「編號!」上士大吼道:「爲什麽看編號?」

　　「要確定,」新兵溫和地解釋說:「我是在擦自己的槍。」

(E)

　　人稱美國是個人種混雜的國家，這一特徵沒有比在戰時更能清楚地看出。二次世界大戰期間，原國籍不同的美國人爭先恐後地參加陸軍報効他們的國家。

　　一個四十歲的愛爾蘭人，出現在辦徵募的軍官面前。愛爾蘭人急於想應徵。此人壯碩有力，而且健康非常良好，會是個好新兵，但是規定徵兵的最高年齡是三十八歲，滿腔熱血的愛國者大失所望。

"Listen, are you *sure* of your age?" asked the officer meaningfully. "Suppose you go home and think it over,❹ and then come back tomorrow."

The following day the Irishman reappeared. "Well, how old are you now?" the officer asked.

"I was wrong yesterday," was the reply. "Sure, I'm thirty-eight; it's me old mother who's forty."

註釋: ❶ melting pot: 人種混雜的國家
　　　❷ sign up: 應徵加入軍隊
　　　❸ husky: 强健的／結實的
　　　❹ think over: 仔細考慮

「聽着，你確知你的年齡嗎？」軍官意味深長地問：「不妨回家去仔細想想，明天再來。」

第二天愛爾蘭人又出現了。「唔，現在你是幾歲啊？」軍官問道。

答話是：「我昨天弄錯了，的確，我是三十八歲，我的老媽才是四十歲。」

31. MUSIC WORLD

(A)

IT IS SAID THAT one characteristic of genius is tempera-
ment. Arturo Toscanini, renowned❶ orchestra conductor, was
especially noted for his short temper with the musicians
under his direction.

Once, while conducting the Philharmonic Symphony
Society in New York, he found fault with the harpist.❷ In
this particular symphony, the harp had only one note to
play, and during the first rehearsal,❸ the harpist plucked
the wrong string.

After receiving a piece of Toscanini's mind,❹ the
unfortunate musician could not stay calm enough to play
the correct note all that day. Nor could he the next day,
nor throughout the entire rehearsal period, despite the
maestro's shouts of fury.

When the day came for the actual broadcast, the
harpist entered the stage to find his colleagues in a state
of amusement. Investigating the cause of their mirth, he
found that only one string remained on his instrument—
the one he had to play that afternoon.

註釋: ❶ renowned: 著名的
　　　 ❷ harpist: 豎琴手
　　　 ❸ rehearsal: 排演／預演
　　　 ❹ give a piece of one's mind: 直率地說

音 樂 世 界

（A）

　　人說天才的特徵之一是有脾氣。著名的管絃樂隊指揮阿都羅‧托斯卡尼尼尤以對他所指揮的樂師發脾氣而聞名。

　　有一次，當他在紐約指揮交響樂團時，他發現豎琴手有錯。在這一支交響樂曲中，豎琴只須彈一個音符，但在第一次排演時，豎琴手撥錯了絃。

　　被托斯卡尼尼指責了以後，不幸的樂師那一整天便無法鎮靜下來彈對那個音符。第二天和整個排演期間他還是一樣。雖然大師憤怒地叫喊也是無用。

　　到了眞正廣播的一天來臨時，豎琴手走上臺發現他的隊友樣子挺樂。他察看他們高興的原因，發現他的樂器上只剩了一根絃—就是那天下午他應該彈的那一根。

(B)

Not everyone can appreciate the finer qualities of modern art. At one performance of the music of a contemporary serious composer, the audience was blasted with six xylo-phones,❶ ten pianos, a fire-alarm siren,❷ an airplane propeller, and a number of automobile horns.

The music was loud, to say the least,❸ but the audi-ence listened patiently for a while for the sake of❹ art. The sound became louder and louder, however, and most mem-bers of the audience felt a mounting dismay.

Eventually, one gentleman in the front could take it no longer. He tied his white handkerchief to his cane and lifted his "surrender" signal toward the orchestra. His fellow listeners roared in amused agreement.

註釋: ❶ xylophone: 木琴
　　　❷ fire-alarm siren: 火警警報器
　　　❸ to say the least: 至少可以說
　　　❹ for the sake of: 為了／因□的緣故

◆◆◆◆◆◆◆◆◆◆◆◆◆◆◆◆◆◆◆◆

(C)

In the mid-1800s, Franz Liszt traveled widely, playing his own and other people's music for admiring audiences. His mastery of the art of playing the piano gained him fame as the greatest virtuoso❶ of his day.

(**B**)

不是每個人都能欣賞現代藝術的優點。在一次嚴肅的現代作曲家音樂演奏會上，聽眾遭到六架木琴、十架鋼琴、一個火警警報器、一個飛機螺旋槳和幾個汽車喇叭的響聲轟震。

音樂至少可以說是太響了，但聽眾爲了藝術忍耐着聽了一會。不過響聲越來越大，大多數聽眾不舒服的感覺也愈見高漲。

最後，前排的一位男士吃不消了。他把他的白手帕繫在手杖上，向樂隊舉起了「投降」的信號。和他一起聽音樂的人哄然大笑高興地表示同感。

(**C**)

在一八〇〇年代中期，弗朗玆・李斯特到處旅行，爲仰慕他的聽眾，演奏他自己和其他人作的樂曲。他彈奏鋼琴的熟練技巧，贏得了當代最偉大名家的美譽。

On one occasion, Liszt was invited to the court of Nicholas I, Emperor of Russia. Pleased with the invitation, Liszt developed an outstanding program of music for the evening. But even as Liszt began to play, the Emperor began conferring with an aide sitting nearby.

Liszt, who was very keenly aware of the distraction,❷ nevertheless continued playing. He expected that the Emperor would soon fall silent, but Nicholas continued talking. Liszt finally gave up❸ playing.

It was then that the Emperor stopped his conversation and sent an aide to the piano to find out why Liszt had halted the performance. The musician was furious, but knew he had to be discreet. His reply was, "When the Czar speaks, everyone should be silent."

Nicholas nodded, and was indeed silent for the rest of the evening.

註釋: ❶ virtuoso: 名家／音樂名手
　　　❷ distraction: 干擾
　　　❸ give up: 中止／停止／放棄

◆◆◆◆◆◆◆◆◆◆◆◆◆◆◆◆◆◆

(D)

JACK SILVERS wanted to entertain his mother, so he bought two front-row-center seats and accompanied her to the Barnum & Bailey Circus. His mother watched all the acts disdainfully. Nothing seemed to please her. She wasn't at

有一次，李斯特被邀到俄皇尼哥拉斯一世的宮廷。李斯特對這次邀請感到高興，爲當晚準備了一個出色的音樂節目。但是等到李斯特已經開始演奏，皇帝却和坐在他旁邊的副官商談起來。

李斯特很敏銳地察覺到這項干擾，但他還是繼續演奏下去。他希望皇帝一下就不再作聲，但尼哥拉斯還是繼續講話。最後李斯特中止了演奏。

這時皇帝才停止談話，並且差了一名副官到鋼琴邊去看看李斯特爲什麼中止了演奏。音樂家非常惱怒，但他知道他必須謹愼。他的答話是，「俄皇講話時，人人都應該靜默。」

尼哥拉斯點點頭，後來便眞的一晚上都沒有再作聲。

(D)

傑克・希爾佛斯想讓他媽媽高興，買了兩張前排中央坐位的票，陪她去巴南姆・培萊馬戲團。他媽媽看所有的表演都瞧不上眼，好像沒有什麼東西讓她高興。馴獅人一點也沒有打動她。象跳舞她沒有覺得有趣。對雜技演員她也冷冷地。後來宣

all impressed by the lion tamer; the dancing elephants didn't amuse her; the tumblers❶ left her cold. Then the main act was announced. Hidalgo would walk a tightrope❷ fifty feet in the air while playing a violin.

Jack nudged his mother and said, "Ma, watch this. This is the big one. Don't be frightened. This is gonna be great!"

His mother didn't change her expression. To the applause of the crowd, the man walked across the tightrope playing one of Mozart's minuets in a manner worthy of❸ a concert hall. Then, to everybody's amazement, he took one foot off the tightrope, and standing on tip-toe❹ he played Beethoven's Moonlight Sonata.

Jack Silvers crowed, "Well, Ma, what do you say to that?"

"Well," conceded his mother, "okay...but Heifetz he ain't."

註釋:　❶ tumbler: 雜技演員
　　　　❷ tightrope: （走繩索用的）拉緊的繩索
　　　　❸ worthy of: 足以□的
　　　　❹ on tip-toe: 用腳尖

(E)

BY THE TIME Mozart was three he could play the clavier,❶ and by the age of five he began composing. When this

佈主要的表演上場了，希達爾哥要一面拉提琴一面在五十英尺
高處走繩索。

傑克用肘推推他媽媽說：「媽，看這個。這可是個大節目。
別怕。這是了不起的！」

他媽媽的表情並沒有改變。在觀衆的掌聲中，那人一面以
相當於在音樂廳演奏的姿態演奏莫札特的一首小步舞曲，一面
走繩索。然後，使每個人驚愕的是，他居然從繩索上抬起一隻
腳，用腳尖站着，演奏貝多芬的月光奏鳴曲。

傑克・希爾佛斯得意洋洋地說：「媽，你看那個怎麼樣？」

「噢！」他媽媽讓步說：「還可以……但他可不是海費兹。」

(E)

莫札特三歲時就能彈奏鍵盤樂器，五歲已經開始作曲。當
這位音樂天才終於有了親生的孩子時，他差不多作成了現在認

musical genius finally had children of his own, he was well on the way to having composed the more than six hundred works now to his credit.

One day, Mozart's precocious❷ son, Karl, later to become an accomplished pianist, approached his father.

"Father," said the young boy, "I would like to start writing symphonies. Perhaps you can tell me how."

"The best advice I can give you, Karl," Mozart said, "is to wait until you are older and more experienced, and then try your hand at❸ less ambitious pieces to begin with."

The young man was taken aback.❹ "But Father, you yourself wrote full symphonies when you were considerably younger than I."

"Ah," said Mozart, "but I did so without asking advice."

註釋: ❶ clavier: 鍵盤樂器

❷ precocious: 早熟的

❸ try one's hand at: 試做

❹ be taken aback: 出乎意料／吃驚

◆◇◆◇◆◇◆◇◆◇◆◇◆◇◆◇◆◇◆◇◆

(F)

OPERATIC STAR ENRICO CARUSO told of the time when his car sprang a leak❶ while he was driving through the country.

爲是他光榮的六百多首曲子。

　　一天，莫札特早熟的兒子，日後成爲有才藝鋼琴家的卡爾，走到他父親身旁。

　　「爸爸，」年幼的孩子說：「我想開始作交響樂曲。也許你能告訴我怎樣作。」

　　「卡爾，我能給你最好的意見，」莫札特說：「就是等你長大些，經驗更多些，然後開始試試你的手，去作規模比較小的曲子。」

　　年青人很感覺意外，「可是，爸爸，你比我年紀小很多的時候，就作完整的交響樂曲了。」

　　「啊！」莫札特說：「可是我作曲沒有問人意見呀。」

(F)

　　歌劇明星安利柯・卡魯索曾說有一次他駕車走過鄉下，發生漏油現象。

Unversed❷ in the mechanics of an automobile, Caruso sought help from a nearby farmer, who kindly fixed the car and then invited Caruso to join him for a meal.

Caruso was grateful, and decided to treat the generous man with an impromptu❸ aria.❹ The farmer was astonished at the voice, and asked who the singer was.

"Caruso," bowed the young tenor.

"Think of that!" said the farmer. "Why, I've read about you for years!"

Caruso beamed at the recognition. "Yes?" he said.

"Oh yes," exclaimed the farmer. "And to think I've had you sing for me, here in my own kitchen! Caruso, the great, the famous traveler, Robinson Caruso!"

註釋: ❶ spring a leak: 產生漏油 (水) 現象

❷ unverse: 不熟悉

❸ impromptu: 卽興的

❹ aria: 抒情調

　　卡魯索因爲對汽車的機械不熟悉，便向附近的一個農人求援。農人欣然把車修好，並請卡魯索與他共餐。

　　卡魯索感激他，決定唱一曲卽興的抒情調，來酬報這位慷慨的人。

　　農夫聽了歌聲大驚，問歌者是誰。

　　「卡魯索。」年輕的男高音鞠了一躬。

　　「想想看！」農夫說：「噢！我讀到關於你的事已經好多年了！」

　　卡魯索見他認知便微笑了。「是嗎？」他說。

　　「啊，是啊！」農夫大聲說：「想想看，我還讓你唱給我聽，就在我家的厨房裏！卡魯索，偉大的、有名的旅行者，魯賓孫・卡魯索！」

32. NEWSPAPERS

(A)

ONE CUB REPORTER was anxious to leap to fame and glory. He spent every spare moment scouting for stories that might be newsworthy, and one day he came across❶ an event that seemed suitable.

He wired his editor for permission to submit a major report from out of town. The answering wire came back curtly, "Send six hundred words."

This wouldn't allow the reporter to expand his style as he wanted to do, so he tried sending another telegram. "Can't be told in less than twelve hundred words," was the message.

His veteran❷ editor was unsympathetic. He sent back this reply: "Story of creation of world❸ told in six hundred. Try it."

> 註釋:　❶ come across: （偶然）碰見／無意中發現
> 　　　　❷ veteran: 資深的
> 　　　　❸ creation of world: 創世

◆◈◆◈◆◈◆◈◆◈◆◈◆◈◆◈◆◈◆◈◆

報　　　紙

（A）

　　一個初出茅廬的記者很想一躍成名。他把每一分鐘都用來發掘可能有新聞價值的事物。有一天他遇到了一件像是合用的事件。

　　他打電報給他的總編輯請准許他由城外寄交一篇有份量的報導。覆電來得簡略,「寄六百字。」

　　這樣就使得那記者不能隨心所欲地發揮他的風格了。於是他又試拍了一個電報。電文是「無法以少於一千二百字叙述。」

　　他那資深總編輯並不表同情。他拍出了這樣的覆電:「創世故事卽以六百字叙述。試試。」

(B)

REPORTERS SOMETIMES FIND it hard to get appointments with well-known people for interviews. One journalist, however, has developed a can't-fail technique.

"When a secretary asks me, 'What did you wish to speak to him about?' I reply angrily, 'I want to know what he's going to do about my wife!' She puts the call through❶ every time!"

註釋: ❶ put through: 接通 (電話)

◆◆◆◆◆◆◆◆◆◆◆◆◆◆◆◆◆◆◆◆

(C)

ARTHUR BRISBANE was a very hardworking newspaperman whose column❶ was widely acclaimed. But when his employer, William Randolph Hearst, offered to give him a six-months' paid vacation, Brisbane refused.

Hearst was puzzled❷ and asked Brisbane why he did not want the vacation. Brisbane replied, "There are two reasons why I will not accept your generous offer, Mr. Hearst. The first is that if I quit writing my column for half a year, it might affect the circulation❸ of your newspapers."

Then he smiled and winked. "The second reason is that it might *not!*"

註釋: ❶ column: 專欄
    ❷ puzzle: 迷惑
    ❸ circulation: 銷路

(B)

記者往往不易與知名人士約會採訪。但某記者想出一個萬靈的辦法。

「當一位秘書問我，『你想和他談什麼？』時，我就生氣地回答，『我想知道他要把我太太的事怎麼辦！』每次她都會把電話接過去！」

(C)

阿瑟‧布里斯本是一位非常努力工作的記者，他的專欄廣受一般人的歡迎。但是當他的雇主威廉‧蘭道爾夫‧赫斯特給他六個月的休假，並且照常支薪時，他拒絕了。

赫斯特覺得莫明所以，就問布里斯本為什麼不要休假。布里斯本回答說：「赫斯特先生，我不接受您慷慨的提議有兩個理由。第一個理由是，如果我停寫專欄半年，也許會影響你報紙的銷路。」

然後他笑笑，又擠擠眼說：「第二個理由是，也許不會有影響！」

(D)

Perhaps the most important tenet❶ of journalism is to verify all information. Cub❷ reporters learn that rule when they join the staff; veteran editors instill it in their underlings.

After the Civil War, young Mark Twain headed west to begin his literary career as a newspaper journalist. His first editor firmly informed him that the paper would not print any fact if the reporter could not vouch for its veracity.

Covering the society events new reporters are often tested on, Twain came back with this careful report:

"A woman giving the name of Mrs. James Jones, who is reported to be one of the society leaders of the city, is said to have given what purported❸ to be a party yesterday for a number of alleged❹ ladies. The hostess claims to be the wife of a reputed attorney."

註釋: ❶ tenet: 教義
　　　❷ cub: 生手記者／初出茅廬記者
　　　❸ purport: 稱做
　　　❹ alleged: 聲稱的／所謂的

(D)

　　新聞學最重要的敎條，或許就是證實一切消息。初出茅廬的記者，在進入報社就職時獲知這項規定；資深編輯則把它灌輸給他們的屬下。

　　南北戰爭後，馬克·吐溫到西部，開始他新聞記者的寫作生涯。他所遇到的第一位編輯斬釘截鐵地告訴他如果記者不能保證一件事情的眞實性，報社就不會刊印出來。

　　採訪社會新聞的新手記者，常會受到考驗。吐溫交回了如下的一篇謹愼小心的報導：
　　「一位稱爲詹姆斯·鍾斯太太的婦人，據報係市內社會領導人物之一，傳聞昨日曾舉行似可稱爲派對的宴會，邀請若干名女客。女主人自稱係名律師的夫人。」

33. OBESITY

(A)

G. K. Chesterton was a man of ample proportions, whose brilliant humor and love for life made friends even of those who disagreed with his strong religious views.

On one occasion, meeting his friend, George Bernard Shaw, Chesterton gestured toward the playwright's❶ slender frame❷ and said, "Looking at you, Shaw, people would think there was a famine in England."

Eyeing the other's corpulent❸ figure, Shaw replied, "And looking at you, Chesterton, people would think you were the cause of it."

註釋: ❶ playwright: 劇作家
❷ frame: 軀體
❸ corpulent: 肥胖的

◆◆◆◆◆◆◆◆◆◆◆◆◆◆◆◆◆◆◆◆◆

(B)

The great Austrian-American opera contralto Ernestine Schumann-Heink had a rich, full voice, and an expansive❶ figure to match. One time, during a season with the Metropolitan Opera in New York, she joined tenor Enrico Caruso for dinner.

肥　　胖

(A)

　　柴斯特頓是個體型肥大的人，他出色的幽默和對人生的喜愛，使不贊同他強烈宗教觀念的人，也能與他成為朋友。

　　有一次，柴斯特頓遇到他的朋友喬治・巴納德・蕭，對這位劇作家細瘦的身材作了個手勢說：「蕭，人家看着你，會以為英國發生了饑荒。」

　　蕭望了望對方肥胖的身段回答說：「柴斯特頓，人家看着你，會以為你就是饑荒的原因。」

(B)

　　優秀的澳美歌劇女低音歐奈斯汀・舒曼海茵克，擁有一副嘹亮、宏朗的歌喉，也有一個相稱的肥大身材。一次，在紐約大都會歌劇院演出期間，她與男高音安利柯・卡魯索一同晚餐。

The waiter served a modest❷ salad to Caruso, and for Madame Schumann-Heink he brought an enormous❸ steak that filled an entire plate.

Caruso was amazed. "Surely you don't intend to eat that steak all alone?" he asked.

"Of course not," the contralto assured him. "I intend to eat it with potatoes."

註釋: ❶ expansive: 寬濶的
　　　❷ modest: 適度的
　　　❸ enormous: 巨大的

◆◆◆◆◆◆◆◆◆◆◆◆◆◆◆◆◆◆◆

(C)

THE PLUMP❶ YOUNG LADY told all her friends that she was on a crash diet,❷ and often complained of the hardships she was undergoing in fighting the temptations to gorge❸ herself. One day a group of her friends discovered her in a restaurant eating a tremendous steak.

"What's the idea?" they asked. "We thought you were dieting?"

"I am," the young lady replied. "This is simply to give me the strength to continue."

註釋: ❶ plump: 肥胖的／豐滿的
　　　❷ diet: 節食
　　　❸ gorge: 狼吞虎嚥

　　侍者拿了一小盤沙拉給卡魯索，給舒曼海茵克太太却拿了
一塊擺滿整個盤子的大牛排。

　　卡魯索吃了一驚。「你總不會打算單獨吃那塊牛排吧？」
他問。

　　「當然不，」女低音確定地說：「我打算和洋芋一起吃。」

(C)

　　一個豐滿的年青女人告訴所有的朋友說她正在猛烈節食，
而且時常訴苦說正和那想要狼吞虎嚥的誘惑作艱苦鬥爭。有一
天她幾個朋友發現她在一家餐廳吃一塊很大的牛排。

　　「怎麼回事啊？」她們問：「我們還以爲你在節食呢。」

　　「是的，」年青的女人回答說：「這只是爲了給我繼續節食
的力氣呀。」

34. OLD AGE

(A)

GRANDPA JONES, AGE 76, had announced his intention to get married, and his relatives were worried. Mae Belle, his bride-to-be,❶ was only 21.

One of Grandpa's❷ daughters finally laid it on the line.❸ "Gramps, you know we're very concerned. Getting married at your age is definitely a hazard.❹ It could be fatal."❺

"Well," Gramps chuckled, "I wouldn't fret over it. If she dies, I'll simply get married again."

> 註釋: ❶ bride-to-be: 準新娘
> ❷ gramps: 祖父
> ❸ lay on the line: 冒讀言明
> ❹ hazard: 危險／冒險
> ❺ fatal: 致命的

◆◇◆◇◆◇◆◇◆◇◆◇◆◇◆◇◆◇◆

(B)

Three old men were sitting together conversing. One thought a while and then said to the other two oldsters, "Who would you like to be buried with?"

老　　年

(A)

　　七十六歲的鍾斯爺爺宣佈他有意結婚。他的親戚都擔着心。他的準新娘梅貝兒才二十一歲。

　　最後老爺爺的一個女兒放膽把話明說了。「爺爺，你知道我們非常不放心。以你的年紀續婚絕對是冒險。說不定會要了命。」

　　「噢！」爺爺呵呵地笑了。「我不煩這個。她要是死了，我只要再結一次婚就是了。」

(B)

　　三個老人坐在一起聊天。有一個想了一會，然後對其他兩個老頭說：「你們願意和誰葬在一起啊？」

The first said, "With Einstein, because he was one of the greatest geniuses the world has ever seen."

The second one said, "With Franklin Delano Roosevelt, because he was one of the greatest Americans who ever lived."

The third one said, "With Kim Novak."

"What!" said the other two. "You want to be buried with Kim Novak? Why, she's not dead yet!"

"Neither am I," said the third gent.❶

註釋:　❶ gent＝gentleman

◆◆◆◆◆◆◆◆◆◆◆◆◆◆◆◆◆◆◆

(C)

A well-preserved❶ matron❷ was conversing with the philosopher-politician Cicero in ancient Rome. "I am only thirty years old," asserted the woman vainly.

"It must be true," replied the statesman, "for I have heard it these twenty years."

註釋:　❶ well-preserved: 保養得好的
　　　　❷ matron: 年長婦人

◆◆◆◆◆◆◆◆◆◆◆◆◆◆◆◆◆◆◆

第一個說道:「和愛因斯坦，因為他是世人所見到的最偉大天才之一。」

第二個說:「和佛蘭克林·第拉諾·羅斯福，因為他是最偉大的美國人之一。」

第三個說:「和金·露華。」

「什麼！」另兩個說:「你要和金·露華葬在一起？怎麼說，她還沒死啊！」

「我也沒死呀！」第三個男士說。

(C)

在古代羅馬，一位保養得好的年長婦人正和哲學家兼政治家的西賽洛談話。「我才三十歲，」婦人自負地聲言。

「這話一定是真的。」政治家回答說:「因為我已經聽了二十年了。」

(D)

Morris Bloomstein was upset. His father, a good man, was having trouble sleeping at night, and there was nothing the son could do to help. He gave the man ear plugs, pills, warm milk and honey, but nothing worked.

One day, Morris heard about a very expensive hypnotist❶ who claimed he could suggest anything to a person's subconscious.❷ He was especially noted for his work with insomniacs.❸ So Morris called on the man, agreed to pay his huge fee, and made an appointment for him to come to the house.

The hypnotist came, and told Mr. Bloomstein to lie down on the couch. Slowly, he twirled his shiny watch before the man's eyes and spoke gently, softly, soothingly, watching the eyes begin to droop.❹ "Relax, Mr. Bloomstein," he cooed.❺ "Look at the gold watch—watch it move —you are getting sleepy—you are feeling heavy—so sleepy —you can't keep your eyes open—"

Mr. Bloomstein's eyes were closed now, and he was breathing smoothly and deeply. Morris, who was almost asleep himself, tiptoed out of the room with the hypnotist. He wrote him a large check, and showed him to the door with effusive thanks.

(D)

　　摩里斯・布魯姆斯坦心裏煩亂。他父親是個好人，但夜晚難以入睡，而做兒子的也沒有辦法幫忙。他給老人耳塞、藥丸、熱牛奶和蜂蜜，但沒有一樣有用。

　　有一天，摩里斯聽說一個收費很高的催眠術師，自稱能對一個人的潛在意識做任何暗示。他尤其以對不眠症患者有辦法而聞名。於是摩里斯去拜訪此人，同意付給他非常高昂的費用，並約定日期請他到家裏來。

　　催眠術師來了，並叫布魯姆斯坦先生睡在床上。他緩慢地把他閃亮的錶在布先生眼前搖晃，一面輕聲柔和而鎮撫地講着話，一面望着對方的眼皮開始垂下來。「放鬆，布魯姆斯坦先生，」他唧唧咕咕地說：「看着這個金錶——看它動——你睏了——你覺得倦了——睏得厲害——你不能睜着眼睛了——」

　　這時布魯姆斯坦先生的眼睛閉上了，而且呼吸得平順又低沈。摩里斯本人也幾乎要睡着了，便同催眠術師躡手躡脚地走出了房間。他開了一張大額支票，並由衷表示感謝，把催眠術師送到門口。

Then quietly he went back in to where his father lay peacefully. In the semidark room, Morris looked fondly on his father's relaxed face. Then suddenly, the man's eyes flew open and the voice was strong. "Well, Morris, has that crazy guy left already?"

註釋: ❶ hypnotist: 催眠術師
　　　 ❷ subconscious: 潛在意識
　　　 ❸ insomniac: 不眠症患者
　　　 ❹ droop: 下垂
　　　 ❺ coo: 喞喞咕咕地說

◆◆◆◆◆◆◆◆◆◆◆◆◆◆◆◆◆◆◆◆

(E)

When a wonderful old gentleman reached the amazing❶ age of 102, he was invited by a radio station to tell everyone his secret for long life.

His explanation was simple: "Every morning when I get out of bed, I have two choices: to be happy or to be unhappy. I always choose to be happy."

註釋: ❶ amazing：驚人的

　　然後他輕輕地走回他父親安安靜靜躺着的地方。在稍暗的房裏，摩里斯懷着愛意望了望他父親安息的面孔。忽然間，老人的雙眼睜大，以強有力的聲音說：「喂！摩里斯，那個瘋子已經走了嗎？」

(E)

　　有一位了不起的老先生，在活到一百零二歲的驚人高齡時，受到一個廣播電臺的邀請，要他告訴大家他長壽的秘訣。

　　他的說明是簡單的：「每天早上我起床時有兩個選擇：要快活還是不快活。我總是選擇快活。」

(**F**)

One aging justice was acutely conscious of every ache and pain, unhappily anticipating his end through a cloud of hypochondria.❶

One afternoon, he was playing a game of cards with an associate's pretty niece when he suddenly clasped his hands together and turned pale.

"It's come," he said, panic-stricken.❷ "My left side is paralyzed."❸

"Heavens!" worried the girl, rising from the card table to call an ambulance. "Are you sure?"

"Positive," said the judge. "I've been pinching❹ my left leg, and I feel absolutely no sensation."

The girl sat back down in her chair. "Your Honor," she said, "you *wouldn't* have felt it. That was *my* leg you were pinching."

註釋:　❶ hypochondria: 憂鬱症
　　　　❷ panic-stricken: 驚慌失措的
　　　　❸ paralyze: 麻痺
　　　　❹ pinch: 掐

(F)

　　一個年老的推事，對於一點疼痛都非常敏感，經常在憂鬱症的陰影下，愁苦地等着末日來臨。

　　一天下午，他正和一位同事的漂亮侄女玩牌，忽然間合起他的手掌，臉色變爲蒼白。

　　「來了。」他驚慌失措地說：「我的左半身麻痺了。」

　　「天啊！」女孩很擔心，從牌桌上站起來去叫救護車。「眞的嗎？」

　　「確實是的。」推事說：「我一直在掐我的左腿，但我一點感覺都沒有。」

　　女孩坐回她的椅子說：「閣下，您不會有感覺的。您掐的是我的腿。」

35. OLD FRIENDS

A businessman was sitting quietly in a restaurant eating his lunch when suddenly a stranger hailed him.

"Hey there, Weinstein!" shouted the man. "My goodness, what happened to you? You used to be❶ short, now you're tall. You used to be blond, and now you're dark-haired. You used to have blue eyes, and now they're brown!"

The businessman was polite but firm. "I beg your pardon,❷ sir, but my name's not Weinstein."

"My God!" exclaimed the other. "You changed your name, too!"

註釋: ❶ used to be: 過去曾是
　　　❷ I beg your pardon: 對不起／抱歉

老 朋 友

　　一個商人靜靜地坐在一家餐館吃午餐，忽然有個陌生人向他打招呼。

　　「喂，溫斯坦！」那人叫道。「啊呀，你怎麼搞的？以前你矮小，現在高了。以前你是金髮，現在是黑髮了。以前你是藍眼睛，現在是褐色眼睛了！」

　　商人委婉而堅定。「對不起，先生，我的名字不叫溫斯坦。」

　　「天啊！」另一個人喊道：「你連名字也變了！」

36. PANHANDLERS

(A)

THE BLIND MAN was standing in front of❶ a building jiggling❷ his tin cup when a woman stopped and dropped a quarter into the cup.

"God bless you!" the blind man beamed. "I knew you had a kind heart the minute I laid eyes on you."

> 註釋: ❶ in front of: 在□前面
> ❷ jiggle: 輕搖

◆◆◆◆◆◆◆◆◆◆◆◆◆◆◆◆◆◆◆

(B)

A PANHANDLER❶ WALKED up to a gentleman in the street and grabbed him by the lapels.❷ "Gimme❸ a quarter, mister," he said.

"Of all the nerve!" the gentleman declared angrily. "What's the idea of stopping people in the street and asking for money?"

"What do you want me to do," the panhandler replied, "open an office?"

> 註釋: ❶ panhandler: 乞丐
> ❷ lapels: 衣領
> ❸ gimme＝give me 之略

叫 化 子

(A)

　　瞎子站在一座大樓前，搖着他的馬口鐵杯子；這時有一位太太停下來，拿一枚兩毛五的銀幣，投進了杯子。

　　「上帝保佑你！」瞎子笑着說：「我第一眼看到你，就知道你心地仁慈。」

(B)

　　一個乞丐在街上走到一個紳士面前，抓住他的衣領。「先生，給我兩毛五吧！」他說。

　　「神經！」紳士生氣地說：「在街上攔住人要錢，是怎麼搞的？」

　　「你要我怎樣，」乞丐回答說：「開個辦公室？」

(C)

A WEALTHY MAN decided to eat his lunch in the park one day to catch some rays of sun. Suddenly, an old man appeared, dressed in rags.❶

"Mister," entreated❷ the poor man, "I haven't eaten anything for three days."

The rich man kept on eating.

"It's three days, mister, that I haven't eaten."

Still no response.

The beggar made still another try. "You hear—three days that no food has passed my lips."

The rich man was quite obviously annoyed❸ as he put down his sandwich. "It's amazing. You yourself won't eat, yet you won't let me eat either."

註釋: ❶ rags: 破衣服
　　　❷ entreat: 乞求
　　　❸ annoy: 使困惱

(D)

A RAGGED PANHANDLER stopped Calloway on the street and asked for some money for a meal. "I'll tell you what I'll do," Calloway told him, "I'll buy you a drink."

"I don't drink," said the panhandler.

"Well then, I'll buy you a couple of good cigars."

(C)

　　一個有錢人有一天想曬曬太陽，決定在公園裏吃午餐。忽然間，出現了一個穿着破爛衣服的老頭。

　　「先生，」可憐的人乞求說：「我已經三天沒吃東西了。」

　　富人繼續吃着。

　　「有三天了，先生，我都沒吃。」

　　還是毫無反應。

　　乞丐又試了一次。「你聽——三天沒有吃的東西進我的嘴了。」

　　富人顯然很嫌煩地放下他的三明治。「眞奇怪。你自己不肯吃，也不肯讓我吃。」

(D)

　　一個衣着破爛的乞丐在街上擋住卡洛威的去路，向他討錢吃飯。「我來告訴你我要怎麼辦，」卡洛威對他說。「我請你去喝一杯。」

　　「我不喝酒。」乞丐說。

　　「那好吧，我買幾支好雪茄給你。」

"I don't smoke," the panhandler replied. "I just want a little money for something to eat."

"I've got a good tip❶ on a nag❷ in the sixth race this afternoon," Calloway continued. "I'll put up the money, you can take the winnings. How about it?"

"But, sir, I don't gamble," protested the panhandler. "All I want is a little money for a bite to eat."

"I'll tell you what I'll do," Calloway responded. "I'll take you home with me for dinner. I want my wife to meet you because I want her to see what can happen to a man who doesn't drink, smoke or gamble."

註釋: ❶ tip: 秘密消息（貼士）
　　　 ❷ nag: 賽馬

◆◆◆◆◆◆◆◆◆◆◆◆◆◆◆◆◆◆◆

(E)

Mrs. Heckstein was preparing dinner when a beggar came to her door. "Lady, I haven't eaten for three days. Have you got something for me?"

"I haven't got much," said Mrs. Heckstein. "Would you like maybe some noodle soup❶ left from the night before?"

"That would be great!"

"Good! Then come back tomorrow."

註釋: ❶ noodle soup: 麵條湯

「我不抽煙。」乞丐回答說：「我只想要一點錢來吃點東西。」

「今天下午第六場賽馬裏，我對一匹馬有看好的情報。我出錢，你可以拿獎金。怎麼樣？」

「可是，先生，我不賭。」乞丐提出異議說：「我要的只是一點錢，好吃一口東西。」

「我告訴你我要怎麼辦，」卡洛威回答說：「我帶你回家吃晚飯。我要我太太見見你，因爲我要讓她看看一個不喝酒不抽煙不賭博的男人會有什麼樣的遭遇。」

(E)

赫克斯坦太太正在準備晚餐時，一個乞丐來到她門前。「太太，我已經三天沒吃飯了。你有沒有什麼東西給我？」

「我沒有多少，」赫克斯坦太太說：「也許你喜歡隔夜的剩麵湯吧？」

「那太好啦！」
「好！那明天再來吧。」

37. PARENTS & CHILDREN

(A)

Royal fathers often encounter the same problems with their children as other parents.

George V of England was a man who always favored moderation.❶ So when the future Edward VIII was attending university and sent to his father for funds, the King answered with a letter that expounded❷ on the virtues of sound financial management.

He angrily explained that he wanted his son to learn the value of money and become a success in the world. The king sent the letter off, hoping he had taught the boy a useful lesson.

Two days later, he received this reply: "Father, I have taken your advice. Have just sold your letter to a collector❸ for 25 pounds."

註釋: ❶ moderation: 節制
　　　 ❷ expound: 解釋
　　　 ❸ collector: 收藏家

親　　子

(A)

　　做國王的父親，往往遇到和普通人父母與子女間發生的同樣的問題。

　　英國的喬治五世是一個經常贊成節制的人。所以當未來的愛德華八世正在讀大學，寫信給他父親要錢時，這位國王便回了一封信，解釋健全的財務處理的好處。

　　他氣忿地說明他要他兒子知道錢的價值，而在世上做一個成功的人。國王寄出了信，希望他給了孩子一個有用的教訓。

　　兩天後，他接到了這樣的回信：「父親，我聽從了你的意見。剛把你的信以二十五鎊賣給一個收藏家。」

(B)

A father was walking through Central Park pushing his young son along in a baby carriage. The kid was howling uncontrollably. Everybody turned and stared.

The father merely kept repeating very softly, "Take it easy, Merwin. Take it easy.❶ Control yourself."

A woman approached the distressed father. She said, "I am a teacher in a progressive school and I notice the way you handle your child. I must say that I admire the way you keep your temper.❷ A fine looking lad you have in that carriage, Sir. So his name is Merwin."

"Oh, no," corrected the father. "His name is Oliver. *I* am Merwin!"

註釋: ❶ take it easy: 不急／不要緊張

❷ keep one's temper: 忍住怒氣／忍耐

◆◆◆◆◆◆◆◆◆◆◆◆◆◆◆◆◆◆◆

(C)

Mrs. Mandelbaum was on her way out of the supermarket when she ran into her old friend Mrs. Rosenstein. The ladies hadn't seen each other for years, so they had much to catch up on.❶

"Tell me," said Mrs. Rosenstein, "How's your boy David?"

"Oh, David!" cried Mrs. Mandelbaum. "What a son. He's a doctor with a big office!"

(B)

　　一個爸爸推着嬰兒車裏的兒子，穿過中央公園。孩子大聲哭鬧，無法控制。人人都轉過頭注視。

　　爸爸只是輕聲重複說着：「麥文，別急。別急。忍着點。」

　　一個女人走近心煩的爸爸身邊。她說：「我是一個前進的學校的老師。我注意到你對待孩子的辦法，我必須說我很佩服你耐着性子的作法。先生，你那車裏的孩子挺漂亮，他的名字是叫麥文了。」

　　「啊！不。」爸爸糾正說：「他的名字叫奧利佛，我才是麥文。」

(C)

　　曼戴爾包姆太太走出超級市場時，遇到了老朋友羅森史坦太太。兩位太太彼此已多年不見，因此有許多要追述的事。

　　「告訴我！」羅森史坦太太說：「你的男孩大衛怎樣？」

　　「噢，大衛啊！」曼戴爾包姆太太叫道。「了不起的兒子。他是個有大診所的醫生！」

　　「太好了。那賓傑明怎麼樣？」

　　「賓尼啊！他是個律師。他說不定明年還要競選公職呢！」

"Wonderful. And what about Benjamin?"

"Benny! He's a lawyer. He even might run for❷ office next year!"

"Marvelous! And your third son, Mendel?"

"Well, Mendel is still Mendel. Still a tailor." Mrs. Mandelbaum sighed. "I tell you, if it wasn't for Mendel, we'd all be starving!"

註釋: ❶ catch up (on): 趕上
　　　❷ run for: 參加競選

◆◆◆◆◆◆◆◆◆◆◆◆◆◆◆◆◆

(D)

PARENTS OFTEN SPEAK the truth in ways they didn't intend. When actor Charles Coburn first discovered the joys of the theater at a tender age, he saved every penny and used the money to see play after play. His father one day took the boy aside to give him some advice.

"One thing, son, you must never do," he said "Don't go to burlesque❶ houses."

"Why not?" asked Charles.

"Because you would see things you shouldn't," came the vague reply.

Tantalized❷ by thoughts of what he might see, Charles hurried the very next weekend to a nearby burlesque house.

And his father was absolutely right. Charles indeed saw something he shouldn't have seen—his father!

註釋: ❶ burlesque: 脫衣舞／滑稽戲
　　　❷ tantalize: 逗惹／難熬

「好極了！那你的老三，孟代爾呢？」

「噢！孟代爾還是孟代爾。他仍舊是個裁縫。」

曼戴爾包姆太太嘆了一口氣。「我告訴你，如果不是靠孟代爾，我們全要挨餓了。」

(D)

父母常常以他們沒有想到的方式說實話。查爾斯・柯本幼年最初發現對戲劇的喜愛時，他省下每一分錢，用來看一齣又一齣的戲。他爸爸有一天把孩子拉到一邊，給了他一些勸告。

「兒子，有一件事你絕不能做，」他說：「不要到脫衣舞舞廳去。」

「為什麼不能？」查爾斯問。

「因為你會看到不該看的東西。」答話來得含糊。

就在那一個週末，查爾斯忍不住想到底會看見什麼，急忙跑到附近的脫衣舞廳去了。

他的爸爸完全說對了。查爾斯果然看到他不該看的東西——就是他爸爸！

(E)

A FATHER AND HIS SON were walking through the park, and every few steps the little boy would ask another question.

"What is lightning?"

"Why is the sky blue?"

"What makes trains run?" and so on.

To each question his father replied that he didn't know.

"Pop," the boy continued, "do you mind if I ask you all these questions?"

"Not at all,❶ son. Keep right on❷ asking. How else will you ever learn anything?"

註釋: ❶ not at all: 毫不
      ❷ keep on: 繼續／持續

(E)

一個爸爸同他兒子在公園裏散步，每走幾步路小男孩就問一個問題。

「閃電是什麼？」

「爲什麼天是藍色的？」

「是什麼東西讓火車走？」

他的爸爸對每一個問題都回答不知道。

「爸！」男孩繼續說：「我問你這些問題你介意嗎？」

「一點也不，兒子。　繼續問好了。　不然你怎麼學得到東西呢？」

38. POLICE

(A)

In many small villages, some public officials still perform several functions. One constable❶ in a small midwestern town also operates as the local veterinarian.❷

Not too long ago, his wife took an anxious phone call. "Is Mr. Whittaker there?" a hysterical neighbor asked.

"Do you want my husband as a veterinarian or as a constable?" Mrs. Whittaker asked.

"Both!" exclaimed the neighbor. "We can't get our bulldog to open his mouth, and there's a burglar in it!"

註釋:　❶ constable: 警官
　　　　❷ veterinarian: 獸醫

◆◈◆◈◆◈◆◈◆◈◆◈◆◈◆◈◆◈◆

(B)

A COP WAS CROSSING Brooklyn Bridge. There was a man perched on❶ one of the girders,❷ ready to leap.

警　伯

（A）

　　在很多小村莊裏，有些公職人員仍然執行幾種職務。一個中西部小城的警官，也在當地做獸醫的工作。

　　不久以前，他太太接到一通焦急的電話。「維泰克先生在嗎？」一個歇斯特里的鄰居問道。

　　「你要我先生當獸醫呢？還是當警官？」維泰克太太問道。

　　「兩樣都要！」鄰居叫着說。「我們沒辦法讓我們的牛頭狗張嘴，他嘴裏正咬着一個賊呢！」

（B）

　　一個警察走過布魯克林橋。有一個男子坐在欄杆上預備往下跳。

The policeman begged, "Please, mister, if you jump, I will have to jump in after you. It's freezing cold, and while we're waiting for the ambulance to come we'll both catch pneumonia❸ and we'll both die. Please, mister, be a good fellow and go home and hang yourself."

註釋: ❶ perch on: 坐
　　　❷ girder: 桁／樑
　　　❸ pneumonia: 肺炎

◆◆◆◆◆◆◆◆◆◆◆◆◆◆◆◆◆◆

(C)

"SOME YOUNG MAN is trying to get into my room through my window," screamed a spinster into the telephone.

"Sorry, lady," came back the answer, "you've got the fire department.❶ What you want is the police department."

"Oh, no," she pleaded, "I want the fire department. What he needs is a longer ladder."

註釋: ❶ fire department: 消防隊

　　警察乞求道:「求求你，先生，你要是跳的話，我就得跟着你跳。現在天冷得凍冰，在我們等救護車來的時候，我們兩個都會得肺炎，也都會死。求求你，先生，做做好人回家去上吊吧。」

(C)

　　「有個年輕人正要爬窗戶進我的房間。」一個老處女在電話裏喊叫。

　　「對不起，太太。」答話回來了，「你打的是消防隊。你要的是警察局。」

　　「啊，不是。」她反辯說:「我要消防隊。他需要一個更長的梯子。」

39. POLITICS

(A)

LESS THAN THREE YEARS after being elected to Parliament as a Conservative, Winston Churchill braved the voices of the status quo and switched his allegiance to the Liberal opposition. Still only twenty-eight at the time, he had a long political career ahead of him.

He also still had an eye for❶ the ladies, and one day he asked a flirtatious❷ young woman to dinner. It turned out,❸ however, that the lady was brash.❹

"There are two things I don't like about you, Mr. Churchill," said she.

"And what are they?" asked Churchill.

"Your new politics and your mustache," she stated flatly.

"My dear madam, pray do not disturb yourself," Churchill reassured her. "You are not likely to come in contact with either."

註釋: ❶ have an eye for: 有□的眼光／有□的鑑別力
❷ flirtatious: 輕浮的
❸ turn out: 結果爲□
❹ brash: 無禮的

政　　　治

（A）

　　溫斯頓·邱吉爾被選爲保守黨議員後不到三年，便勇敢地面對現狀的主張，轉向反對黨自由黨效忠。那時他才二十八歲，還有一段長的政治前程。

　　他對女人也有眼力。一天他約了一位輕浮的少婦吃晚飯。但後來才發現那位女士沒有禮貌。

　　「你有兩樣東西我不喜歡，邱吉爾先生。」她說。

　　「是什麼東西？」邱吉爾問。
　　「你的新政略跟你的鬍子。」她斷然地說。

　　「我的女士，請你不必煩心。你不像會接觸到這兩樣東西裏的任何一樣。」

(B)

A Mississippian once asked Lincoln why he was so kind to his political enemies. "Why do you try to make friends of them?" he asked. "You know they will only be traitors.❶ You should try to destroy them."

Lincoln responded with generosity and wisdom. "Am I not destroying my enemies when I make them my friends? And a friend is never a traitor."

註釋: ❶ traitor: 叛徒

◆◇◆◇◆◇◆◇◆◇◆◇◆◇◆◇◆◇◆◇◆

(C)

Winston Churchill came into his own❶ while leading England valiantly through World War II. On one occasion, the Prime Minister was headed for the B. B. C. to make a radio address when he met up with❷ an obstinate cab driver.

"Sorry, mister. Ye'll 'ave to get yourself another cab," the driver insisted. "Mr. Churchill is broadcastin' in thirty minutes and I wouldn't miss it for all the fares in London."

Pleased and flattered, Churchill stopped thinking of arguing, and instead took out a onepound bill from his wallet to show how touched he was. But his jaw dropped several inches when the driver's face suddenly brightened.

(B)

有一次一個密西西比人問林肯為什麼他對他的政敵那麼好。「你為什麼要想跟他們做朋友？」他問道。「你知道他們只會變成叛徒，你應該想辦法毀掉他們。」

林肯仁慈而富智慧地回答說：「我和我的敵人做朋友不是就在毀他們嗎？朋友是不會變成叛徒的。」

(C)

溫斯頓‧邱吉爾在勇敢地領導英國度過第二次世界大戰的期間，贏得了他應得的榮譽。有一次，這位首相在前往英國廣播公司作廣播演說時，遇上了一個固執的計程車司機。

「對不起，先生，你得另外叫一部車。」司機堅持說，「邱吉爾先生要在半個鐘頭內廣播，我不要倫敦整個城的車錢，也不能錯過。」

邱吉爾既高興又得意，不願和他爭執，而從皮夾裏拿出一張一鎊的鈔票，表示他有多麼感動。不過當司機的臉上突然綻開笑容時，他只有目瞪口呆的份。

"You're a bit of all right, sir!" the cabbie said, adopting a new set of values. "'Op in,❸ and to'ell❹ with Mr. Churchill."

註釋: ❶ come into one's own: 得到應得的成功（名譽等）

❷ meet up with: 遇見

❸ 'op in＝hop in

❹ to'ell＝to hell

◆❖◆❖◆❖◆❖◆❖◆❖◆❖◆❖◆

(D)

MR. AND MRS. GOLDFINK were worried. All their friends' children had expressed their wishes about what they were going to grow up to be—firemen, policemen, whatever. But their little five-year-old had said nothing about a future career.❶

"I'll tell you what we'll do," said Mr. Goldfink. "We'll put him in a room, all alone, with only a Bible, an apple, and a silver dollar. If he reads the Bible, it means he's going to become a rabbi. If he eats the apple, he wants to be a farmer. And if he plays with the dollar, he's headed for banking."

So the parents put their boy into the room with the three items and waited half an hour. Then they went in to see what he was doing. He was sitting on the Bible, eating the apple, and had put the silver dollar in his pocket!

「你還不錯嘛，先生！」計程車司機說着，採用了一套新的價值觀念。「跳上來吧，去他的邱吉爾先生。」

(D)

葛爾德芬克夫婦憂慮着。他們朋友的孩子都已經表示過長大以後要當什麼——消防隊員、警察或是別的。但是他們的五歲孩子一直沒有說出將來要從事什麼行業。

「告訴你我們要怎麼辦。」葛爾德芬克先生說。「我們把他單獨一個人放在一間房裏，裏面只擺一本聖經、一個蘋果和一枚銀幣。如果他讀聖經，表示他會當牧師。他若吃蘋果，表示他願意當農夫。假如他拿銀幣玩，他就會走向銀行界。」

於是父母二人便把他們的男孩和三件東西放在房裏，等了半小時。然後他們走進去看他在做什麼。他正坐在聖經上吃蘋果，而且已經把銀幣放進了口袋。

"What does that mean?" whispered Mrs. Goldfink to her husband.

"It means he's going to be a politician!"❷

註釋:　❶ career: 職業

　　　　❷ politician: 政客

◆◆◆◆◆◆◆◆◆◆◆◆◆◆◆◆◆◆◆◆◆◆

(E)

Themistocles, political leader of ancient Athens, was once heard to remark that his newborn child ruled Greece. Puzzled, another Athenian asked what the statesman meant.

"Athens dominates❶ all Greece; I dominate Athens; my wife dominates me; and my infant son dominates her," was the reply.

註釋:　❶ dominate: 支配

◆◆◆◆◆◆◆◆◆◆◆◆◆◆◆◆◆◆◆◆◆◆

(F)

Our first President, George Washington, drew a hard line between friendship and business. In one instance, when both a friend and an opponent applied to the President for a particular government position,❶ Washington chose the foe.❷ He felt the latter was better qualified for the job.

Some friends took him to task for his callousness. But Washington replied: "My friend I receive with a cordial

「這表示什麼呢？」葛爾德芬克太太輕聲對她丈夫說。

「這表示他會做一個政客。」

(E)

　　有一次有人聽到古代雅典的政治領袖賽米斯托克利斯說他剛出生的孩子統治了希臘。另外一個雅典人覺得迷惑，便問這位政治家是什麼意思。

　　答覆是：「雅典支配全希臘；我支配雅典；我太太支配我；我的幼兒支配她。」

(F)

　　美國第一任總統喬治·華盛頓把友情和公事劃分得很清楚。有一次，一個朋友和一個敵對者向總統謀求政府中一個特別職位，華盛頓選擇了敵人，他覺得這人比較有資格做那份工作。

　　有一些朋友指責他無情。但華盛頓回答說：「我熱誠地歡迎我朋友，但他雖有許多優點，却不是一個實務家。他的敵對

welcome, but, with all his good qualities, he is not a man of business.❸ His opponent is, with all his hostility to me, a man of business.

"I am not George Washington, but the President of the United States. As George Washington, I would do my friend any kindness in my power, but, as President, I can do nothing."

註釋: ❶ apply for a position: 求職
　　　❷ foe: 敵人
　　　❸ man of business: 實務家

◆◇◆◇◆◇◆◇◆◇◆◇◆◇◆◇◆◇◆

(G)

The power of Benjamin Disraeli's wit was perhaps nowhere evidenced as keenly as in his long-standing antagonism with Parliamentarian William Gladstone.

Once, in a literary debate, Disraeli was asked if there was any difference in usage between the words *misfortune*❶ and *calamity*.❷ He reflected for a moment, then said:

"There is a similarity, but there is also a profound difference. If, let us say, Mr. Gladstone were to fall into the Thames, that would be a misfortune. But if anyone were to pull him out, that would be a calamity."

註釋: ❶ misfortune: 不幸
　　　❷ calamity: 災難

者對我充滿敵意，倒是一個實務家。」

「我不是喬治‧華盛頓，而是美國總統。做喬治‧華盛頓，我會盡我能力所及給我朋友幫忙，但做總統，我就無能爲力了。」

(G)

邊傑明‧狄斯萊利的機智，大約是在他與威廉‧葛拉得斯東議員長期間的對立中，表露得最强烈了。

有一次，在一項文學的討論中，有人問狄斯萊利「不幸」與「災難」兩字用法的差異。他想了一下後說道：

「有相似的地方，但也有很大的差異。假如，我們說，葛拉得斯東先生要是掉進了泰晤士河，那會是不幸。但是倘若有人要把他拉上來，那就會是災難了。」

40. PRAISE & FLATTERY

(A)

VOLTAIRE was famous for his humanistic philosophy, but his penchant❶ for satire❷ also proved him an admirable wit.

Once he was told that a man he had praised was speaking poorly of him.

"Is that so?" Voltaire responded. "Well, perhaps we are both wrong."

> 註釋： ❶ penchant: 傾向／嗜好
>
> ❷ satire: 諷刺

◆◆◆◆◆◆◆◆◆◆◆◆◆◆◆◆◆◆◆

(B)

Dramatist George Bernard Shaw was a keen wit, but he didn't always come out on top.❶

One time, American actress Cornelia Otis Skinner was widely acclaimed for her performance in Shaw's *Candida.* The playwright sent her a telegram stating, "Excellent. Greatest."

The actress was so honored, she wired back, "Undeserving such praise."

讚美與奉承

(A)

　　伏爾泰以他的人道主義哲學聞名，而他嗜好諷刺也表現他具有可欽佩的機智。

　　一次有人告訴他一個他曾經稱讚過的人在貶低他。

　　「是嗎？」伏爾泰答道：「那，或許我們兩個都錯了。」

(B)

　　戲劇家喬治‧蕭伯納是個有銳利機智的人，但他不見得經常佔上風。

　　一次，美國女演員柯尼麗亞‧奧提斯‧史基納因在蕭的「坎狄達」一劇中表演而廣獲讚賞。這位劇作家拍了一個電報給她稱：「傑出，偉大之至。」

　　女演員至感光榮，回電稱：「不敢當如此讚譽。」

Humorously, Shaw sent another cable which said, "I meant the play."

Miss Skinner was annoyed. She retorted❷ by wire, "So did I."

註釋: ❶ come out on top: 勝利
　　　❷ retort: 反駁

蕭幽默地又拍了一個電報說:「我是指戲。」

史基納小姐感到困擾,回電反駁說:「我也是。」

41. PREGNANCY & CHILDBIRTH

(A)

A PRETTY YOUNG GIRL was rushed to the hospital for the delivery of her child. Her boyfriend Larry waited anxiously downstairs. The delivery was extremely long and painful.

When it was all over,❶ the girl sighed and said: "If this is what married life is like, go downstairs and tell Larry our engagement❷ is off!"

註釋: ❶ all over: 全完
　　　❷ engagement: 婚約

◆◇◆◇◆◇◆◇◆◇◆◇◆◇◆◇◆◇◆

(B)

"MRS. SMITH," the doctor told the woman he had just examined, "I have good news for you."

"I'm glad to hear that," the young lady replied, "but I'm *Miss* Smith."

"Miss Smith," the doctor went right on, "I have bad news for you."

懷孕與產子

(A)

一個漂亮女郎要生孩子，被人趕忙送進醫院。她的男友賴利焦急地在樓下等候。生產非常慢而痛苦。

等到一切完畢之後，女郎嘆口氣說：「如果婚姻生活就是這個樣子，到樓下去告訴賴利我們的婚約取消了。」

(B)

「史密斯太太。」醫生對他剛剛檢查過的女人說：「我有好消息告訴你。」

「我高興聽。」年青的女人回答說：「不過我是史密斯小姐。」

「史密斯小姐。」醫生立刻接下去說：「我有壞消息告訴你。」

42.　PSYCHIATRISTS

(A)

The lady told the psychiatrist,❶ "My husband thinks I'm crazy just because I like pancakes."

"But there's nothing wrong with that," said the doctor. "I like pancakes❷ myself."

"Do you?" cried the lady in delight. "Then you must come up some time. I have six trunks full."

註釋:　❶ psychiatrist: 精神病醫師
　　　　❷ pancake: 烤餅（班戟）

❖❖❖❖❖❖❖❖❖❖❖❖❖❖❖❖❖❖

(B)

"DOCTOR," COMPLAINED the distraught❶ mother, "I don't know what to do. My son insists on emptying ashtrays."❷

"Well," said the doctor, "that's not unusual."

"Yes, but in his *mouth?*"

註釋:　❶ distraught: 煩惱的
　　　　❷ ashtrays: 煙灰缸

❖❖❖❖❖❖❖❖❖❖❖❖❖❖❖❖❖❖

精神病醫生

(A)

　　一位太太告訴精神病醫師說:「我丈夫只因為我喜歡烤餅就認為我發瘋了。」

　　「可是那也沒什麼不對呀!」醫生說:「我本身也喜歡烤餅。」

　　「是嗎?」那太太高興地叫道:「那你幾時一定要來,我有滿滿的六大箱呢。」

(B)

　　「大夫!」煩惱的媽媽埋怨說:「我不知道該怎辦?我兒子一定要倒煙灰缸。」

　　「噢!」醫生說:「那並不奇怪啊。」

　　「是,可是倒在他嘴裏呢?」

(C)

TWO EMINENT PSYCHIATRISTS, one 40 years old, the other over 70, occupied offices in the same building. At the end of a long day, they rode down in the elevator together. The younger man appeared completely done in,❶ and he noted that his senior was still quite fresh.

"I don't understand," said the younger, "how you can listen to patients from morning to night and still look so spry."

The old psychiatrist shrugged his shoulders and replied, "Who listens?"

註釋: ❶ done in: 使動彈不得

(D)

A WIDE-EYED❶ CHARACTER who was convinced he was Napoleon burst into❷ a psychiatrist's office, thrust his hand inside his coat, and declared, "It isn't myself I've come to see you about, Doctor. It's my wife Josephine. She thinks she's Mrs. Richardson."

註釋: ❶ wide-eyed: 天眞的
　　　❷ burst into: 衝進／闖入

(C)

　　兩個有名的精神病醫生，一個四十歲，一個七十歲，在同一棟樓裏設有診所。在結束了一長天之後，他們同搭電梯下樓。年青的顯得完全累壞了，而他看出年長的那位倒還相當有精神。

　　「我不明白。」年青的說：「你從早到晚聽病人說話，看上去精神還能這麼好。」

　　年老的精神病醫生聳聳肩回答道：「誰聽呀？」

(D)

　　一個自以為他是拿破崙的天眞人物，衝進一個精神病醫生的診所，把手插入他的上衣，宣稱道：「大夫，我不是為了我自己來看你的，是我太太約瑟芬。她以為她是李查遜太太。」

(E)

"MY POOR HUSBAND," the woman sighed to her psychoan-alyst❶, clutching her husband's hand. "He's convinced he's a parking meter."

The analyst regarded the silent, woebegone❷ fellow and asked, "Why doesn't he say something for himself? Can't he talk?"

"How can he," the wife shrugged, "with all those coins in his mouth?"

註釋: ❶ psychoanalyst: 心理分析家
      ❷ woebegone: 憂愁的

(E)

　　「我可憐的丈夫，」婦人抓着她丈夫的手，對心理分析家嘆息：「他確信他是一架停車計費機。」

　　心理分析家望着那沈默又憂愁的人問道：「他爲什麼不替自己說些什麼呢？他不能講話嗎？」

　　「他怎能講？」妻子聳聳肩，「他嘴裏有那麼多硬幣。」

43. PUBLIC SPEAKING

DR. GEORGE HARRIS, president of Amherst College, had prepared a long speech to give to returning upper classmen the day before school began. The welcoming lecture was the only event scheduled that day for the students, and they grew restless in their seats and gazed longingly at the warm autumn sunshine pouring through the windows.

Dr. Harris himself thought of the golf links as he reluctantly launched into his prepared recitation, but after several minutes he gave up.❶

"I intended to give you some advice," he said, "but now I remember how much is left over❷ from last year unused." He left the auditorium to thunderous applause.

註釋: ❶ give up: 放棄
　　　❷ leave over: 剩下／留下

演　　說

　　阿姆赫斯特大學的校長喬治‧哈利斯博士準備了一篇長演講辭，爲了在開學前一天講給返校的高年級學生聽。那一天爲學生安排的節目，只有這項歡迎演說，而學生們坐在位子上却漸漸地心不定起來，並且熱望地注視着由窗戶照射進來的溫暖的秋天陽光。

　　哈利斯博士本人在勉强開始他準備好的講話時，在想着高爾夫球場，但是過了幾分鐘之後，他放棄了。

　　「我本想給你們一些忠告。」他說：「可是現在我記起去年的還剩下多少沒有用過。」他離開禮堂，響起了如雷掌聲。

44. RELIGION & CLERGYMEN

(A)

Three missionaries working in different parts of the world came together one year to compare notes.❶

"I've converted seventy-five percent of my tribe's members," bragged the first one, "and in addition to those saved souls, we've also built a church and a schoolhouse."

The second missionary was not to be outdone.❷ "In my area, I've converted ninety percent of the natives," he said, "and in addition we've built a church, a schoolhouse, and a hospital."

Then they turned to❸ the third missionary. "Aren't you in an area of cannibals?" he was asked. "Have you persuaded them to give it up?"

"Well, it's a long process," said the third missionary slowly. Then he brightened. "But I have gotten them to❹ use knives and forks!"

註釋：　❶ compare notes: 交換意見
　　　　❷ outdo: 超越／勝於
　　　　❸ turn to: 訊問
　　　　❹ get to: 總算能够／逐漸

宗敎與敎士

(A)

　　在世界不同地區工作的三個傳敎士，有一年來到一起，交換意見。

　　「我已經使我那部落百分之七十五的人改信基督敎，」第一個誇口說：「除了這些被拯救的人之外，我們還蓋了一座敎堂和一棟校舍。」

　　第二個傳敎士不甘落後。「在我那地區裏，我使百分之九十的土著改信了基督敎，」他說：「此外我們蓋了一座敎堂、一棟校舍和一所醫院。」

　　然後他們轉向第三個傳敎士。「你不是在食人族的區域裏嗎？」他被問道：「你有沒有說服他們不再吃人呢？」

　　「哦，這個過程是長的，」第三個傳敎士緩慢地說。然後他顯得高興起來，「可是我已經逐漸讓他們使用刀叉了。」

(B)

In the old country, there was a rabbi who traveled from village to village. In each town he would hold services, and then stay for several hours while the congregation offered him their simple fare and asked questions.

The rabbi's means of transportation was a horse cart, driven by a sturdy, kindly fellow who admired the rabbi greatly. On every visit, after services, while the rabbi was being surrounded by the congregants, the driver would sit by patiently in the synagogue❶ and listen.

After many years, the driver felt bold enough to ask the rabbi to grant one request.❷ Just once, he'd like to feel the thrill of adulation. Wouldn't the rabbi trade❸ places with him just once.

The rabbi wanted to please his loyal driver and granted the request.

The next day, the pair visited a new town. The rabbi and the driver exchanged garments. The rabbi quietly sat in the corner of the synagogue while the crowd gathered around the driver to feed him handsomely, and ask him questions. The driver handled the services and the questions very well for he had listened to his beloved rabbi for many years and he was entirely familiar with the stock❹ questions.

Suddenly, a student arose and posed a complicated philosophical problem. The townsfolk turned to the driver, expecting a profound reply. But the driver knew he was stumped.

(B)

從前在鄉下，有一個猶太教的牧師，一個村落一個村落的走動。在每個鎮上，他都會舉行禮拜儀式，然後停留幾小時，其間會衆獻出他們微少的費用，並提出問題。

牧師的交通工具是一輛二輪馬車，車伕是個粗壯親切的人，對牧師非常敬佩。每到一處訪問，禮拜儀式之後，牧師被會衆包圍時，車伕便耐心地坐在教堂一邊聽着。

許多年之後，車伕覺得可以大膽請牧師答應他一個要求了。只要一次，他想嘗嘗被人奉承的快感，牧師可否就和他調換一次位子。

牧師想讓他忠心的車伕高興，便答應了請求。

第二天，兩人訪問了一個新的小鎮，牧師和車伕換穿了衣服。群衆聚集在車伕周圍慷慨解囊，並問他問題的時候，牧師便靜靜地坐在教堂角落裏。車伕把禮拜儀式和問題處理得很好，因爲他已經聽他所愛的牧師講了好多年，而且對那些普通問題完全熟悉了。

忽然間，有個學生站起來，提出了一個複雜的哲學上的問題。鎮民轉向車伕，期望得到深奧的答覆，但是車伕知道他栽了筋斗。

He hesitated for just a moment, and then he scoffed, "Young man, I am amazed that you should ask such a simple question. Why, even my driver, who is not well-versed❺ in the Talmud,❻ can answer that. And just to show you, we'll ask him!"

註釋:　❶ synagogue: 猶太教會堂
　　　　❷ grant a request: 答應請求
　　　　❸ trade: 交換
　　　　❹ stock: 普通／平凡
　　　　❺ well-versed: 精通
　　　　❻ Talmud: 猶太法典

◆◇◆◇◆◇◆◇◆◇◆◇◆◇◆◇◆

(C)

ORATING ON HELL-FIRE, the minister vividly described the sufferings of the damned.❶ The congregation sat in rapt attention as he eloquently described Dante's inferno.❷ At the climax of his sermon, he quoted from the gospel:

"On that day, there will be a weeping and a wailing and a gnashing of teeth."❸

In the silence a toothless old lady stood up from one of the pews❹ at the back and shouted, "But some of us have no teeth."

"On that day," the minister roared, "teeth will be provided."

註釋:　❶ damned: 墮入地獄的人
　　　　❷ Dante's inferno: 但丁"神曲"中的地獄
　　　　❸ gnashing of teeth: 咬牙切齒
　　　　❹ pew: 教會的座席

他只猶豫了一下，然後嘲笑着說:「年青人，你會問這麼一個簡單的問題我很驚奇。對了，連我的車伕——他並不精通猶太法典——都能回答。爲了給你看看，我們去問他！」

(C)

牧師在講述地獄之火時，生動的描寫着墮入地獄的人所受的苦難。當他能言善道地描寫但丁的地獄，會衆坐着聽得出神。他說教到達高潮，引用了福音中的話:

「那一天，將有悲泣、哭號和咬牙切齒。」

在安靜中，一個沒有牙的老太太從後面座席上站起來大聲說道:「可是我們有些人沒有牙啊。」

「到那天，」牧師吼道:「會供應牙的。」

(D)

As a boy, Woodrow Wilson worshipped his minister father and was overjoyed when the stern man would allow him to come along on visits through the parish.

Later, when he was President, Wilson laughingly recalled the time when his father had taken him to see a neighbor. Seeing the horse and buggy❶ that had brought the minister and his son, the concerned neighbor wondered aloud, "Reverend, how is it that you're so thin and gaunt,❷ while your horse is so fat and sleek?"❸

The Reverend began a modest reply, but before he could say two words, his outspoken❹ son announced to the parishioner's❺ dismay, "Probably because my father feeds the horse, and the congregation feeds my father."

> 註釋: ❶ buggy: 四輪單（雙）座馬車
> ❷ gaunt: 瘦削的
> ❸ sleek: 有光澤
> ❹ outspoken: 坦率的
> ❺ parishioner: 教區民

(E)

A much-loved rabbi died a peaceful death, and his soul rose swiftly to heaven.

There, the rabbi was warmly greeted by hosts of angels. They wanted to honor him by dressing him in

(D)

小時候，伍德羮・威爾遜崇拜他的牧師父親。在這位嚴肅的人准許他隨同去訪問敎區的時候，他簡直高興得不得了。

後來，當他做了總統，威爾遜笑着回憶他父親帶他去看一個鄰居的事。鄰居看到載牧師父子來的馬和馬車，便關心而疑惑地大聲問道：「牧師，你這麼瘦又憔悴，而你的馬倒這麼胖又有光澤，是怎麼回事啊？」

牧師開始作謙虛的答覆，但他還沒有說到兩個字，他坦率的兒子便直說出令這位敎區民狼狽的話：「大槪是因爲我父親餵養馬，而會衆養我父親的關係。」

(E)

一位非常受人敬愛的牧師安祥地死了。他的靈魂很快地昇上了天。

在天上，牧師受到一群群天使熱烈的歡迎。他們要爲他穿上華服，帶領他走過金的街道，以示禮遇，因爲他曾是一個很好

finery and escorting him through the golden streets, for he had been such a fine man. But the rabbi, inexplicably, wouldn't participate. He covered his face with his hands, and fled from the midst of the celebrations.

Astonished, the angels brought the rabbi before God himself. "My child," said the Lord, "it is on record that you have lived entirely in accord with❶ My wishes, and yet you refuse the honors that have, most fittingly, been prepared for you. Why?"

"Oh, Most Holy One," replied the rabbi, prostrating❷ himself, "I am not as deserving❸ as You think. Somewhere along the way I must have sinned, for my son, heedless of my example and of my precepts, turned Christian."

"Alas, I understand entirely and I forgive," said God. "I had the same trouble myself."

註釋:　❶ in accord with: 與□一致
　　　　❷ prostrate: 伏地
　　　　❸ deserving: 該受／獎賞

◆◆◆◆◆◆◆◆◆◆◆◆◆◆◆◆◆◆◆◆

(F)

A WOWAN WENT to confession and told the priest she was having an affair.❶

"This must be at least❷ the tenth time you've told me this story, the priest sighed. "Are you still involved with❸ that man?"

的人。但是不知何故，牧師不肯參與。他用手遮住臉，在慶祝聚會當中逃跑了。

天使們大爲驚異，把牧師帶到上帝的面前。「我的孩子，」主說：「記錄上說你的生活完全符合我的願望，但你却不肯接受爲你準備得最恰當的榮譽，爲什麼呢？」

「啊，最神聖的一位，」牧師伏在地上回答說：「我並不如您所想的那樣該受獎賞。我一定是在什麼地方犯了罪，因爲我的兒子不注意我的榜樣和訓誡，變成了基督徒。」

「啊呀，我完全了解也原諒你，」上帝說：「我自己也有過同樣的麻煩。」

(F)
　　一位婦人到牧師那裏去懺悔，並且告訴他說她有過戀愛事件。
　　「你跟我說這個故事這一定至少是第十次了，」牧師嘆了一口氣。「你還同那個男人有關連嗎？」

"Oh, no, Father," she replied, "I just like to talk about it."

註釋:　❶ affair: 戀愛事件

　　　 ❷ at least: 至少

　　　 ❸ involved with: 有關連

「啊，沒有，神父，」她回答說：「我只是喜歡說它罷了。」

45. RESTAURANTS

(A)

Two men sat down in a restaurant and ordered their main dishes. Then they closed their menus. The waiter said, "Thank you, gentlemen. And would any of you wish a beverage❶ with your meal?"

One man said, "Well, I usually have coffee, but today I think I'll have a glass of milk."

The other man said, "That sounds good. I'll have milk, too. But make sure the glass is clean!"

"Very good," said the waiter, and he left.

Soon he came back with a tray and two glasses of milk, and said, "Here you are,❷ gentlemen. Now which one asked for the clean glass?"

註釋：❶ beverage: 飲料
　　　❷ here you are: 這裡便是（拿東西交付對方）

◆◆◆◆◆◆◆◆◆◆◆◆◆◆◆◆◆◆◆

(B)

Steinberg had been having his lunch in the same Lower East Side❶ restaurant for 20 years. Every day, he left his office at noon, went to the restaurant, and ordered a bowl of chicken soup. Never a change.

餐　　館

(A)

　　兩位男士在餐館坐下來點了他們的主菜。然後他們便把菜單合了起來。侍者說:「謝謝你們，先生。你們那位要不要一樣飲料來配餐？」

　　一個人說:「噢，我平常喝咖啡，不過今天我想我要一杯牛奶吧。」

　　另一個人說:「不錯，我也要牛奶。但注意杯子一定要乾淨!」

　　「很好,」侍者說着就走開了。

　　不多時他拿着一個托盤和兩杯牛奶回來說:「這兒就是，先生。那麼是哪位要乾淨杯子的？」

(B)

　　史坦伯在紐約曼哈坦區東南部的同一家餐館吃午飯已經有二十年了。他每天中午離開辦公室，到餐館去，叫一碗雞湯。從來沒有變過。

But one day Steinberg called the waiter back after receiving his soup.

"Yes, Mr. Steinberg?" inquired the waiter.

"Waiter, please taste this soup."

"What do you mean, taste the soup? For 20 years you've been eating the same chicken soup here, every day, yes? Has it ever been any different?"

Steinberg ignored the waiter's comments. "Please, taste this soup," he repeated.

"Mr. Steinberg, what's the *matter* with you?❷ *I* know what the chicken soup tastes like!"

"Taste the soup!" Steinberg demanded.

"All right, all right, I'll taste. Where's the spoon?"

"Aha!" cried Steinberg.

註釋: ❶ Lower East Side: 紐約曼哈坦區東南部（下層階級住宅區）
　　　❷ what's the matter with you: 你怎麼啦

◆◆◆◆◆◆◆◆◆◆◆◆◆◆◆◆◆◆◆

(C)

A gentleman in a restaurant called the waiter back to his table as soon as❶ his meal was served.

"Why is this chicken missing❷ a leg?" he demanded of the waiter.

"I guess it was in a fight, sir," the waiter shrugged.

　　但是有一天史坦伯在拿到他的雞湯之後，把侍者叫了回來。

　　「噢，史坦伯先生？」侍者問道。
　　「夥計，嚐嚐這個湯。」
　　「嚐這個湯，你是什麼意思？你二十年每天都在這裏吃一樣的雞湯，是吧？有過什麼不一樣的地方嗎？」

　　史坦伯不理會侍者的話。「請你嚐嚐這湯，」他重複說。

　　「史坦伯先生，你是怎麼一回事啊？我知道雞湯是什麼味道！」
　　「嚐嚐湯！」史坦伯命令道。
　　「好吧，好吧，我嚐。湯匙在那兒啊？」
　　「啊哈！」史坦伯叫道。

(C)

　　一位餐館裏的男士，在他的菜端上來時，立刻把侍者叫回他的餐桌旁。
　　「為什麼這隻雞少了一條腿？」他問侍者。
　　「我猜是在打鬪中少的吧，先生！」侍者聳聳肩。

"Well then," the diner replied, "take it back and bring me the winner."

註釋: ❶ as soon as: 立卽
　　　❷ missing: 不足的／不見了的

◆◆◆◆◆◆◆◆◆◆◆◆◆◆◆◆◆◆◆◆

(D)

TWO FELLOWS MET at noon one day for lunch. One ordered chicken soup; the other, borscht.❶

The waiter brought one bowl of chicken noodle soup and one bowl of potato soup.

"I didn't have any more borscht," he said. "I brought you potato soup instead. Try it, it's good."

So the man tasted the soup and loved it. "It's great. The best I ever had!" And he offered some to his companion.

"It *is* good," said the other man. "Waiter, since it's so good, why didn't you bring *me* some potato soup?"

The waiter was offended. "Say, mister," he said, "did you order borscht?"

註釋: ❶ borscht: （俄式蔬菜肉湯）羅宋湯

◆◆◆◆◆◆◆◆◆◆◆◆◆◆◆◆◆◆◆◆

「那好吧！」吃客回答說：「把牠拿回去，把打贏的那隻給我。」

(D)

一天中午有兩個人會面去吃午飯。一個叫了雞湯；另一個叫了羅宋湯。

侍者端來一碗麵條雞湯和一碗洋芋湯。

「我沒有羅宋湯了，」 他說：「我改拿了洋芋湯給你。 試試看，好吃哦。」

於是那人嚐了湯， 而且很喜歡。「好極了， 是我喝過的最好的！」他給了一些給他的同伴。

「好吃！」另一個人說：「夥計，既然這麼好吃，你為什麼不給我拿一些洋芋湯來呢？」

侍者不高興了。「咦！先生，」他說：「你叫羅宋湯了嗎？」

(E)

"LET ME HAVE a turkey sandwich," Wilbur told the man at the delicatessen❶ counter.

"Sorry, we don't have turkey today," was the reply.

"Then gimme a chicken sandwich," said Wilbur.

"Don't be ridiculous," the counter man chuckled. "If I had chicken, wouldn't I have given you a turkey sandwich?"

註釋：　❶ delicatessen: 熱菜店（熟食店）

◆◆◆◆◆◆◆◆◆◆◆◆◆◆◆◆◆◆◆

(F)

In the posh❶ restaurant, a waiter brought out a bowl of soup and placed it before a distinguished patron who was reading a newspaper. With hardly a glance up from his paper, the patron declared, "Not hot enough, bring it back."

The waiter brought another plateful. Again the patron spoke, "Not hot enough."

Another plate was brought—and again the patron sent it back without touching it.

Finally the exasperated waiter said, "Are you sure it isn't hot enough?"

"Absolutely," cracked❷ the patron. "It isn't hot enough as long as❸ you can keep your thumb in it."

註釋：　❶ posh: 漂亮／優雅
　　　　❷ crack: 大聲說
　　　　❸ as long as: 只要

(E)

「給我一份火雞三明治,」威爾伯對熱食店櫃枱上的人說。

回答是:「抱歉，我們今天沒有火雞。」

「那就給我一份雞三明治吧！」威爾伯說。

「別傻了，」櫃枱上的人吃吃地笑了。「如果我有雞，我還會不給你火雞三明治嗎？」

(F)

在一間漂亮餐館裏，侍者端出一碗湯，放在正在看報的一位高尚顧客面前。顧客幾乎沒有把視線從報紙移開朝上看一眼，便宣稱道:「不够熱，拿回去。」

侍者又拿來了一盤湯。顧客又說道:「不够熱。」

另一盤湯拿來了——而顧客又沒有碰就把它退了回去。

最後惱怒的侍者說:「湯是眞的不够熱嗎？」

「絕對是，」顧客大聲說:「只要你能把大拇指放在裏面，湯就不够熱。」

(G)

A CUSTOMER IN the cafe called the waiter to his table and asked, "Is this tea or coffee? It tastes like cough medicine."

"Well, if it tastes like cough medicine, it must be tea," the waiter replied. "Our coffee tastes like turpentine."❶

註釋: ❶ turpentine: 松節油

(H)

A HEALTH INSPECTOR walked into a seedy❶-looking restaurant and asked for❷ the proprietor.

"I notice a sign outside that you're serving rabbit stew today. Is it all rabbit?"

"Well, actually it isn't," the proprietor had to admit. "There's a little horsemeat in it too."

"How much horsemeat?" quizzed❸ the inspector.

"I swear it's a fifty-fifty mixture," the proprietor replied. "One horse and one rabbit."

註釋: ❶ seedy: 難看／不體面的
      ❷ ask for: 找
      ❸ quizz: 質問

(G)

一位顧客在咖啡店裏把侍者叫到他枱子旁邊問道:「這是茶還是咖啡？味道像咳嗽藥。」

「噢！如果味道像咳嗽藥，一定是茶了,」侍者回答道:「我們的咖啡味道像松節油。」

(H)

一個衞生檢查員走進一間樣子不體面的餐館，要找店東。

「我在外面看到一塊牌子說你們今天供應燉兔肉。是全兔肉嗎？」

「哦！其實不是,」店東不得不承認。「也有一點馬肉。」

「多少馬肉？」檢查員質問道。

「我發誓是一牛一牛混合的,」店東答道: 「一匹馬和一隻兔子。」

46. SERVANTS

A successful young architect lived with his wife in a large Westchester ranch❶ house, served dutifully by a Scandinavian❷ cook, whom everyone praised as the best in town. One day, the cook, in tears, approached the lady of the house and told her: "I'm sorry, Madam, but I must leave on the first of the month."

"But why?" demanded the wife. "I thought you liked it here." The cook then bashfully explained that she had met a handsome soldier a few months before, and would soon be expecting a child. Eager to hold on to❸ the talented cook, the wife immediately called her husband, then told the cook: "We've decided to adopt your baby."

A few months later, a daughter appeared upon the scene. The architect legally adopted her, and all was calm for another year, when the cook announced once again that she was leaving—this time due to an encounter with a young sailor. The architect and his wife discussed the matter, then told the cook: "It's not right to bring up a child alone. We'll adopt your second baby."

After the arrival of a darling little boy, all went smoothly for another two years, when the maid resigned again. The wife gasped, "Don't tell me that this time you met a Marine."

僕　　役

　　一個有成就的年青建築師和他太太住在威斯特徹斯特的牧場房屋裏，由一個北歐人厨師忠實地侍候着；這個厨師人人都誇讚說是城裏最好的。一天，厨師流着眼淚走近女主人身旁，告訴她說：「對不起，太太，我這個月一號一定要走了。」

　　「可是爲什麼呢？」太太問道：「我以爲你喜歡這裏。」於是厨師害羞地解釋說她幾個月前遇到了一個漂亮的兵，並且她不久便要生孩子了。太太一心想留住能幹的厨師，立刻叫她丈夫來，然後告訴厨師說：「我們已經決定領養你的嬰孩。」

　　幾個月後，一個女兒出現在幕前了。建築師合法地領養了她，一切平靜地過了一年，厨師再度宣稱她要走了——這回是因爲她遇上了一個水兵。建築師和他太太商量了這件事，然後告訴厨師說：「一個人單獨養育一個孩子是不對的。我們來領養你第二個嬰孩吧。」

　　一個可愛的男孩到來之後，一切順利地又過了兩年，厨師又辭職了。太太喘口氣說：「這回該不會是你遇到了一個陸戰隊員吧？」

"Oh, no, ma'am," replied the cook. "I'm resigning because I simply cannot cook for such a big family."

註釋: ❶ ranch (house): 農場／牧場

　　　 ❷ Scandinavian: 北歐人

　　　 ❸ hold on to: 維持住

　　「哦！不是，太太，」厨師回答說：「我辭職是因爲我實在不能給這麼一大家人燒飯了。」

47. SHIPS

The excursion boat❶ had sprung a leak and was sinking fast. As the passengers prepared to abandon ship, the captain stood at the helm❷ and shouted: "Does anyone here know how to pray?"

One of the passengers shouted back: "I do!"

"Well, you pray, "the captain replied, "and the rest of us will put on the life belts.❸ We're one shy."❹

註釋: ❶ excursion boat: 遊覽船
　　　❷ helm: 舵輪
　　　❸ life belt: 救生帶
　　　❹ shy: 缺少

船

　　遊覽船出現了一個漏洞，很快地在往下沈。當乘客準備棄船時，船長站在舵輪旁叫道:「這裏有人知道怎樣禱告嗎？」

　　一個旅客喊道:「我知道！」
　　「好吧，你禱告吧！」船長回答說:「我們其餘的人穿上救生帶。我們缺少了一條。」

48. SHOW BUSINESS

(A)

GEORGE BERNARD SHAW'S writings made sharp points with which not everyone agreed. Shaw was proud of his general acclaim, but he learned early to deal with his critics.

On opening night, one of his new plays was greeted with such favor that the audience called for❶ him to take a bow. Suffused with pride, Shaw took several. But then one rowdy❷ member of the audience called out loudly, "Shaw, your play stinks!"❸

The audience held its breath in horror. Shaw hesitated briefly, then said, "My friend, I agree with you completely. But what are we two against this great majority?" And the audience before him thundered its approval.

註釋: ❶ call for: 要求
　　　❷ rowdy: 粗暴的／胡鬧的
　　　❸ stink: 聞出臭氣

(B)

A New York producer was delighted that Bidú Sayao, Brazilian opera star, was willing to sign a contract with

演藝生涯

(A)

蕭伯納的作品有些尖刻的地方，不是每個人都贊同的。一般人的喝采他引以為豪，不過他也早就學會去對付批評他的人。

他的一齣新戲首演的夜晚，受到大好評，觀衆要求他上臺鞠躬。蕭躊躇滿志地鞠了幾個躬。可是後來觀衆之中有一個胡鬧的人大聲叫道：「蕭，你的戲好臭！」

觀衆恐怖地屏着息。蕭稍稍遲疑了一下，然後說道：「朋友，我完全與你同感。可是面對這樣的多數，我們兩個又算得了什麼呢？」於是在他前面的觀衆，響起了如雷的贊同掌聲。

(B)

一個紐約的製作人很高興巴西的歌劇明星碧杜・沙亞奧願意同他公司簽訂合約。他請她飛來紐約商定細節。

his company. He had her flown to New York to work out❶ the details.

Accompanied by her mother, the star smiled as she entered the producer's office. As he outlined the financial arrangements, however, Miss Sayao's mother tapped the girl's arm and spoke into her ear. The smile vanished, and the opera star shook her head.

The old woman didn't speak much English, and the producer didn't understand Portuguese, but he immediately upped the figure he had offered. Yet the mother tapped again, whispered more intensely, and the girl shook her head once more.

The producer offered more money several times in quick succession,❷ but could not get the girl to stop shaking her head "no." Finally, he could go no higher. "That is my best offer," he asserted. "Either you sign at this figure or the contract is off."

"But certainly!" the girl agreed. "Of course I sign."

The mother tapped her daughter once more. Bidú lowered her eyes, then, and asked, "My mother wants to know, please—where is the ladies' room?"

註釋: ❶ work out: 努力完成／詳細擬定
　　　❷ in succession: 連續着

這位明星由母親陪同，微笑着走進了製作人的辦公室。但是當他大略述說了金錢上的安排時，沙亞奧小姐的母親便拍拍女郎的手臂，在她耳邊說了些話。微笑消失了，歌劇明星搖了搖頭。

老太太不會講多少英語，而製作人也不懂葡萄牙語，但他立刻提高了他願出的價錢。不過媽媽又拍了一次，更急切地輕聲講話，女郎則再度搖了搖頭。

製作人連續幾次增加他願出的價錢，但不能使女郎停止搖頭說「不。」最後，他無法再提高了。「那是我最好的出價了，」他聲明道：「要嘛你就按這個數目簽字，否則合約就吹了。」

「那當然！」女郎同意道。「我當然簽字。」
媽媽又拍了她女兒一次。碧杜放低了視線，然後問道：「我媽媽想知道，請問——洗手間在那裏？」

(C)

ONCE OSCAR WILDE set out❶ to review a play that others had greeted as a fiasco. When asked how he thought the play had fared, Wilde replied, "The play was a great success, but the audience was a failure."

註釋: ❶ set out: 出發

(C)

　　有一次奧斯卡‧王爾德出去評審一齣旁人認爲大失敗的戲劇。當有人問他覺得那齣戲怎麼樣時，王爾德回答道:「戲是大成功，但觀衆是失敗了。」

49. SMOKING

A **VENDOR❶** **STANDING** on the street offered cigars at 5¢ apiece. A man strode up to him, paid his nickel, lit the cigar, took a puff, and then began to cough violently.

"What kind of rot❷ are you selling me?" he yelled "this cigar is positively putrid!"❸

The vendor looked sympathetically, then pointed to three cases of merchandise lying next to him: "You're complaining! You only bought one! *Look at all I bought!*"

註釋: ❶ Vendor: 行商小販
　　　❷ rot: 腐敗物
　　　❸ putrid: 腐敗的

吸　　烟

　　站在街邊的一個小販在賣一支五分錢的雪茄煙。一個男子大步走到他前面，付了他的五分鎳幣，點燃雪茄，吸了一口，然後猛咳起來。

　　「你賣給我的是什麼爛貨？」他喊道：「這支雪茄簡直爛透了！」

　　小販同情地望了望，然後指着放他旁邊的三箱貨說：「你還埋怨！你只買了一支！看看我買的這些！」

50. TEACHERS & STUDENTS

(A)

A MATH TEACHER asked, "Joey, if your father borrowed $300 and promised to pay back $15 a week, how much would he owe❶ at the end of ten weeks?"

"Three hundred dollars," the boy replied quickly.

"I'm afraid you don't know your lesson very well," he teacher scolded.❷

"Well," Joey replied, "I'm afraid you don't know my father."

註釋: ❶ owe: 欠
　　　❷ scold: 責罵

(B)

THE TEACHER IN A tenement❶ district sent Mrs. Cohen a candid note which read:

"Your son Abie stinks. Give him a bath."

Mrs. Cohen's reply was just as direct. "My son Abie ain't no rose. Don't smell him. Learn him."

註釋: ❶ tenement: 租房

師　　　生

（A）

　　一位算術老師問道：「喬埃，　如果你爸爸借了三百塊錢，而且答應每個禮拜還十五塊，十個禮拜之後他還欠多少？」

　　「三百塊！」男孩回答得快。
　　「恐怕你不大懂你的功課，」老師責怪說。

　　「啊！」喬埃答道：「恐怕是你不懂我爸爸。」

（B）

　　一個租屋住戶區的老師寫了一張不客氣的字條給寇漢太太說：「令郎阿比有臭味。給他洗個澡。」

　　寇漢太太的答覆也同樣直接了當。「小兒阿比不是玫瑰花。不要聞他。教他。」

(C)

Young Samuel arrived home after his first day at Hebrew school.

"Well," said his mother, "tell me what you learned today."

"Today we learned about Moses," answered Samuel.

"And what do you know about Moses?"

"Well, he was this general, see. And he got all the Jews together in formation❶ and marched them out of Egypt, with General Pharaoh's Egyptians hot❷ on their trail.❸ And then in front of him, there was the Red Sea blocking his path. So Moses ordered bombs dropped, and bang! The waters parted just long enough for the Jews to get across.❹ And when the Egyptians followed, they were all drowned."

The mother was aghast. "Is that how they teach the story of Moses nowadays?"

"No, Mom," answered Sammy. "But if I told you the story the way the teacher told it to us, you'd never believe it."

註釋:　❶ formation: 編隊
　　　　❷ hot: 接近
　　　　❸ on the trail of: 跟蹤／追趕
　　　　❹ get across: 越過／渡過

(C)

　　小薩姆埃兒第一天上猶太學校後回到家裏。

　　「好啦，」他媽媽說:「告訴我你今天學了什麼。」

　　「今天我們學了關於摩西的事，」薩姆埃兒答道。
　　「那你知道摩西一些什麼事呢?」
　　「噢!他是這個將軍，知道吧。他把所有猶太人編成隊，讓他們行軍走出埃及，埃及法老將軍的人就在後面緊緊追趕。後來紅海在前面擋住了他的去路。於是摩西就下令丟炸彈，轟隆!水分開來剛好夠猶太人渡過。等到埃及人跟來時，他們就全都淹死了。」

　　媽媽目瞪口呆。「他們現在是這樣教摩西的故事的嗎?」

　　「不，媽。」薩米回答說。「可是我若照老師講給我們聽的樣子給你講這故事，你是絕對不會相信的。」

(D)

THE TEACHER ASKED little Morris whether the world was round or flat.

　　Morris thought a moment, then said, "I guess it's neither, because my dad's always saying that it's crooked."❶

　　註釋: ❶ crooked: 歪的／扭的

(D)

老師問小摩里斯地球是圓的還是扁的。

摩里斯想了一下，然後說：「我想都不是，因爲我爸爸常說世界是歪扭的。」

51. THEFT & LOSS

(A)

Nat was upset.❶ "Irving, I lost my wallet and it had three hundred dollars in it!" he lamented.❷

Irving tried to help Nat think. "Did you look everywhere for❸ it?" he asked. "What about your coat pockets?"

Nat said, "Sure I looked. I tried all my coat pockets, all my vest pockets, my front pants pockets, and my left hip pocket—and it just isn't anywhere."

"Your left hip pocket? Why don't you try your right hip pocket?" asked Irving.

"Well," replied Nat, "that's the last pocket I have."

"So?"

"So, if I look in that pocket and if I don't find the wallet there, I'll drop dead!"

註釋: ❶ upset: 煩亂
　　　❷ lament: 悲嘆
　　　❸ look for: 尋找

賊 與 失 物

(A)

　　納特很煩亂。「歐文，我丟了皮夾，裏面有三百塊錢！」他傷心地說。

　　歐文試幫納特想。「你到處都找過了嗎？」他問：「你上衣的口袋怎樣？」

　　納特說：「我當然看過。我試過我上衣所有的口袋、我背心所有的口袋、我褲子前面的口袋和我屁股左邊的口袋——就是到處都沒有。」

　　「你屁股左邊的口袋？你為什麼不試試右邊的口袋呢？」歐文問道。

　　「噢！」納特回答說：「那是我最後一個口袋了。」

　　「因此怎樣？」

　　「因此如果我看了那個口袋又在裏面找不到皮夾，那我就要倒地而亡了。」

(B)

THE YOUNG NEWLYWEDS had just moved into their new apartment when they received a pleasant surprise in the mail—a pair of tickets to the best show in town. The donor had not sent his name, and for the rest of the day the newlyweds wondered who had sent them the coveted❶ tickets.

After enjoying the show, the young couple arrived home, and found that a burglar had broken in❷ and stolen all their wedding presents. A note read:"Hope you enjoyed the show."

註釋：　❶ coveted: 垂涎／妄想
　　　　❷ break in: 闖入

◆◆◆◆◆◆◆◆◆◆◆◆◆◆◆◆◆◆◆◆◆

(C)

A HOUSEWIFE LEFT HOME for the day and locked the house up❶ tightly, leaving a note on the door for the grocer:❷ "All out. Don't leave anything."

On returning home, she found her house burglarized and all her valuables stolen.

On the note to the grocer was added: "Thanks. We haven't left much."

註釋：　❶ lock up: 上鎖
　　　　❷ grocer: 食品雜貨商

(B)

　　一對年青新婚夫婦剛剛搬進他們的新公寓，便在信件中得到一份驚喜——兩張鎮上最好的戲票。送票人並沒有署名；那一天新婚夫婦就一直覺得奇怪，是誰寄給他們那令人垂涎的戲票。

　　在欣賞過戲之後，年青夫婦回到家，發現有賊闖進去偷掉了他們全部的結婚禮物。一張紙條上寫着：「希望你們高興看那齣戲。」

(C)

　　一個家庭主婦要離開家一天，把屋門緊緊上了鎖，並在門上留了個字條給食品店的人：「都已外出。不要留下東西。」

　　回到家，她發現有賊侵入屋內，把她所有值錢的東西都偷光了。

　　在給食品店的字條上，加了：「多謝。我們沒有留下多少。」

(D)

A South American dictator was building a luxurious retreat❶ for himself and his wife just outside his capital city. A rigid guard was established around the project to prevent the theft of valuable materials.

Each day at noon, the same workman appeared at the exit gate with a wheelbarrow❷ loaded with dirt. The suspicious guard searched the dirt carefully each day, and even had it analyzed by a chemist to make sure nothing was being concealed. But the guard could find nothing to substantiate his suspicion, and, day after day, he let the workman pass.

A few years later, the guard met the same workman in the capital. The laborer was evidently enjoying great prosperity, and the guard was curious. "Now that it's all over,"❸ pleaded the guard, "just what were you stealing every day on that construction project?"

The workman grinned❹ and answered,"Wheelbarrows."

註釋: ❶ retreat: 隱退所
　　 ❷ wheelbarrow: 手推車
　　 ❸ all over: 結束
　　 ❹ grin: 露齒而笑

(D)

一個南美的獨裁者，在他首都城外為他和他妻子建造一座豪華的退隱時住所。工程的周圍設了嚴密的警衛，以防值錢的材料被偷。

每天中午，同一個工人總會推着裝滿泥土的手推車，出現在出口的大門處。多疑的警衛每天都小心搜查泥土，甚至把泥土給化學家分析，以確定沒有東西藏在裏面。但是警衛沒有找到任何足以證實他懷疑的東西，而一天又一天，他都讓那工人通過了。

幾年後，警衛在首都遇到了同一個工人。這個工人顯然大大的發達了，警衛覺得好奇。「反正一切都過去了，」警衛懇求道：「你在那個建築工程裏，每天偷的到底是什麼呢？」

工人笑了笑回答說：「手推車。」

52. TRAINS

When the conductor on a rickety❶ old Tennessee line came through the car to collect the tickets, an old fellow in the back couldn't find his in any pocket. The conductor stood waiting until a man across the aisle❷ laughed and said, "Cal, you've got the dang❸ thing in your teeth." The conductor then punched❹ the ticket and continued down the aisle.

"Cal, you're sure getting absent-minded," the man across the aisle chuckled.❺

"Absent-minded my foot❻!" Cal whispered with a wink. "I was chewing off last year's date."

註釋: ❶ rickety: 搖擺的
　　　❷ aisle: (列車內座位之間) 通道
　　　❸ dang＝darn＝damn: 該死／可惡／討厭
　　　❹ punch: 打孔
　　　❺ chuckle: 吃吃地笑
　　　❻ my foot: 笑話

火　車

在一條搖搖晃晃的老田納西鐵路線的車上，車掌走來收票時，後面的一個老先生在他任何一個口袋，都找不到票。

車掌站着等待，直到過道對面的一個人笑笑說：「卡爾，你把那倒霉東西咬着呢。」車掌把票打了孔，繼續走下過道。

「卡爾，你真變得心不在焉了，」過道對面的人吃吃地笑着。

「心不在焉，笑話！」卡爾擠擠眼輕聲說：「我是在咬掉去年的日期呀。」

53. TRAVEL & VACATIONS

CUSTOMS OFFICIALS are like doctors-they see people's most personal belongings, and they have to be prepared for anything.

One woman at Kennedy Airport insisted she had brought nothing abroad.❶

"Are you quite sure that you have nothing to declare?"❷ the customs agent asked her.

"Absolutely sure," she said firmly.

"Am I to understand, then," smiled the agent, "that the fur tail hanging from under your dress is your own?"

註釋: ❶ aboard: 在船（火車，飛機，巴士）上
　　　 ❷ declare: 申報（納稅物品）

旅遊與休假

海關官員像醫生——他們看人們私有的所有物，也要有準備面對任何事情。

一個女人在甘酒廸機場堅決說她沒有帶任何東西登機。

「你相當確定沒有要申報的東西嗎？」海關人員問她。

「絕對確定，」她堅定地說。
「那麼，我是不是應該認為，」那人員微笑着，「從你衣服下面垂下來的毛尾巴是你自己的呢？」

54. VANITY

(A)

At a recent dinner party, a woman spoke to the man seated on her right and said that men were much vainer❶ than women. The gentleman thought that idea was preposterous,❷ and that vanity was a trait❸ unheard of in men.

The woman said, "I'll prove it to you. Watch."

Then she raised her voice several degrees❹ and said quite firmly, "It's a shame that most intelligent and sensitive men attach so little importance to❺ the way they dress. Why, right this minute, the most cultivated man in this room is wearing the most clumsily knotted tie."

She easily won her point when every man's hand suddenly flew to his neck.

註釋: ❶ vain: 愛虛榮
　　　❷ preposterous: 荒謬/可笑/不合理
　　　❸ trait: 特性
　　　❹ degree: 音階的度
　　　❺ attach importance to: 對□重視

虛　　榮

(A)

　　在最近一次晚宴上，一個女人同坐在她右邊的男人談話，並說男人比女人虛榮心更强。男士認爲那種想法是荒謬的，而且虛榮在男人中是從未聽過的特性。

　　女人說，「我來給你證明，看着。」

　　於是她把聲音提高幾度，相當堅定地說，「最聰明而有感性的男人這麽不重視他們衣着的樣式，太丟面子了。對了，就在此刻，這個房間裏最有教養的人就繫着一條打得最笨拙的領帶。」

　　當每個男人的手忽然飛向他衣領時，她的論點輕易取勝了。

(B)

One awkward❶ adolescent❷ visited her priest and shyly told him she thought she'd committed the sin of vanity.

"What makes you think that?" the Father inquired.

"Every morning when I look into the mirror," she said, embarrassed, "I think how beautiful I am."

"Never fear, my girl," said the strict Father. "That isn't a sin; its only a mistake."

釋註: ❶ awkward: 尷尬的
　　　❷ adolescent 青年/年輕女性

◆◇◆◇◆◇◆◇◆◇◆◇◆◇◆◇◆◇◆◇◆

(C)

The choice of words we make is often of utmost importance to our listeners.

Trying to reach a top-shelf book one day, Napoleon was stymied❶ by his inability to stretch his arm far enough. An extremely tall marshal came to his aid❷ and took the book down, saying to his Emperor, "Permit me, sir—I am higher than Your Majesty."

Napoleon angrily grumbled, "Marshal, you are longer."

註釋: ❶ stymy: 妨礙/阻撓
　　　❷ come to (a person's) aid: 援助（某人）

(B)

一個尷尬的年青女性去看她的神父，並且羞怯地告訴他她認為犯了虛榮的罪。

「是什麼讓你那麼想的？」

「每天早上當我看鏡子裏的時候，」她困窘地說，「我就想我有多美。」

「絕不要怕，我的孩子，」嚴厲的神父說。

「那不是罪，只是一項錯誤。」

(C)

我們選擇用語對聽的人往往有極大的重要性。

有一天，拿破崙想伸手去拿書架頂層的書，却因手臂伸不到那麼遠而受到阻撓。一個非常高的元帥來幫他忙把書拿了下來，一面對他皇帝說，「請讓我來──我比陛下高。」

拿破崙惱怒地抱怨道，「元帥，你是比較長。」

55. WAGERS

(A)

The twenty-ninth President of the United States, Calvin Coolidge, was a reticent❶ man, never known for scintillating❷ conversation.

A socialite❸ once sat next to him at a party and babbled,❹ "Oh, Mr. President, do you know I made a bet today that I would get more than two words out of you?"

Maintaining his reserve❺, Coolidge responded quietly, "You lose."

註釋: ❶ reticent: 沈默/無言
　　　❷ scintilate: 閃放光芒
　　　❸ socialite: 名士
　　　❹ babble: 嘮叨
　　　❺ reserve: 寡言/節制

◆◆◆◆◆◆◆◆◆◆◆◆◆◆◆◆◆◆

(B)

An army lieutenant asked his superior, Captain Smith, to reprimand❶ a private who spent his free time teaching the other men the art of gambling. The captain was a sober, moral man, and if anyone could straighten Jones out,❷ he could.

打　　賭

（A）

　　美國第廿九任總統卡爾文・柯立芝是一個沈默寡言的人，從未有人聽說他有談笑風生的時候。

　　在一次宴會中，有一個名士坐在他旁邊嘮叨說，「哦，總統先生，你知道嗎？我今天和朋友打一個賭說我會讓你講兩個以上的字。」

　　柯立芝保持着他的寡言，靜靜地說，「你輸。」

（B）

　　一個陸軍中尉請求他的長官史密斯上尉，懲戒一個在空閒時教旁人如何賭博的士兵。上尉是個嚴謹、規矩的人，如果有人能矯正鍾斯，他就能。

Private Jones entered Captain Smith's quarters❸ with a neatly pressed uniform, newly shined shoes, and a smart salute.

"At ease,❹ young man," began Captain Smith. "Now, is it true that you're a gambler?"

"Sir," answered Jones respectfully, "it's a habit I just can't seem to lose. Why, I'll bet you ten dollars right now that you have a mole❺ on your left shoulder."

The captain saw this as a chance to make a point.❻ He knew Private Jones rarely lost a bet, but he also knew he had no mole. If he could force the private to lose, he might be able to reform him. Laying down the ten dollars, he stripped off❼ his shirt and pointed to his smooth left shoulder.

"See there, young man? No mole," Smith asserted. "Let that be a lesson to you. Gambling simply does not pay.❽ Private Jones stared at his shoes dolefully, and after being dismissed, went back to his barracks.❾

Captain Smith immediately called in the lieutenant and told him what had happened. Puffed up❿ with pride, he couldn't understand the lieutenant's silence. "What's the matter?" Smith asked finally. "Aren't you pleased?"

"No, sir," the lieutenant said slowly. "You see, on the way to your quarters Jones bet me twenty-five dollars he'd have the shirt off your back in five minutes."

註釋:　❶ reprimand: 懲戒/譴責
　　　　❷ straighten out: 矯正

　　士兵鍾斯穿着燙得平整的制服和剛擦亮的鞋，帥氣的敬着禮走進史密斯上尉的營房。

　　「稍息，年青人，」史密斯上尉開始道。「聽說你是個賭徒，是眞的嗎？」

　　「長官，」鍾斯恭恭敬敬地回答說。「這是個習慣，我好像就是不能丟掉。來，我現在就和您賭十塊錢，賭您的左肩上有一顆痣。」

　　上尉認爲這是一個使對方瞭解道理的機會。他知道士兵鍾斯很少打賭打輸，但他也知道他沒有痣。他如果能逼這士兵賭輸，他或許能使他改邪歸正。放下十塊錢，他便脫掉襯衫，指指他光滑的左肩。

　　「看到那裏吧，年青人？沒有痣。」史密斯斷言道。「讓這件事給你一個教訓吧。賭博是完全不值得的。」士兵鍾斯悄然看看他的鞋，退出之後，回到了他的營房。

　　史密斯上尉立刻把中尉召來，告訴他發生了什麼事。他驕傲得意，不明白中尉爲什麼沈默不語。「怎麼回事啊？」史密斯終於發問道。「你不高興嗎？」

　　「不是的，長官。」中尉慢慢地說。「你知道，在到你營房來的路上，鍾斯和我賭二十五塊錢，賭在五分鐘內讓你從背上脫下襯衫。」

❸ quarters: 軍營/宿舍

❹ at ease: 稍息

❺ mole: 黑痣

❻ make a point: 使聽者徹底了解論旨

❼ strip off: 脫掉

❽ pay: 值得/有利/合算 (does not pay: 不值得)

❾ barracks: 軍營

❿ puff up with: 爲□自滿